A LOST PAIGE

L. ROSE

CHAPTER ONE
PAIGE

It had been two weeks since we buried my hellhound. Two weeks and I couldn't mend the gaping hole in my chest. It remained raw and open from the loss—from the thought of never seeing Ezra, who had been there from the start. He'd been by my side, right from when I climbed out of the grave the former ghoul queen had buried me in. He'd taught me to hunt, to feed, to live, and to fight.

How was I supposed to go on without him?

He wasn't just any hellhound. He'd been mine. He was smart, cheeky, and fierce.

I wanted him back.

Back rolling his eyes or laughing at me. Back with his knowing looks every time I got aroused by my bonded mates.

Yasmin, my sister, sat on the couch beside me. She tucked a stray blonde strand behind my ear. "You don't have to do this," she told me.

But I did.

I wanted to go to the dungeons where Patrice, Odin, and Barrett were being held. Where they'd been suffering and starving. I wanted to go in there so I could question them myself.

I'd let myself have time after burying Ezra to mourn, and even though my heart remained broken, I wanted answers. They'd caused this hole inside me. They'd killed my hellhound. I wanted them to pay a hell of a lot more than they were. They'd taken someone I cared for away from me. There was no chance I'd let that go unpunished.

"I do," I answered, my voice cold.

"Paige, please let your mates handle it," she pleaded.

I stood, shaking my head. "I'm the queen, Yasmin. If I want answers, I will do the work to get them. They took Ezra. They broke a piece of me. They will suffer by my hand, and it will show others what will happen if they try to take from me again."

After a moment, she stood, nodded, and took me in for a hug. "Okay," she whispered.

After I returned her embrace, I faced my mates at the door to my family's suite and walked to them. Alex was the first to reach out and take my hand. They had been amazing since... since we lost Ezra. I hadn't as yet finalized the bond with Nate or Alex, like I already had with Asher and Thorn. But they never pushed me. They knew I wasn't in the right frame of mind. Instead, my sweet, amazing men held me when I cried, comforting me all the time. They even distracted me when I needed it. Nate did it by pissing me off. Alex when he showed me some magic. Thorn and Asher when they spoke of things happening around the castle. They'd even worked out with me daily on new fighting tactics. Nate had been the one to suggest it, saying I needed to gain some muscle on my puny body. We'd sparred right away after that comment, and I realized how good it felt. Not only did it take my mind off things, but my body also ached in a way that exhausted me. It was that night I slept for the first time.

My mates were perfect.

Especially when they were dealing with an overemotional woman.

But I wasn't sure I would ever get over losing Ezra. The

loss had darkened me inside, and I held onto it, that blackness, because I refused to move on and forget him.

As Asher opened the door, he called back to Yasmin, "We'll have her back soon."

"Take care of her," she said.

"Always," Thorn replied before he stepped out the door first. Then I went, still holding Alex's hand. Asher and Nate walked out after me. Outside of the room, Thorn's men, my personal guards, surrounded us as we silently made our way down underneath the castle's floors and into the cold, damp dungeons.

Some of the guards stayed at the entrance while one opened the locked gated door and we walked in. He shut the door and stayed by it. We traveled to the end of the hall. I wanted to start with Patrice first. I had a feeling she would be weaker than Odin or Barrett. Along the way, I happened to glance into a cell and saw Malvina, the ghoul who'd disrespected me and had wanted Thorn for herself. I sent a questioning glance at Thorn, who was looking at me. He said, "No one speaks to you that way, my queen."

I nodded. "Get one of the guards to see if she's learned her lesson. If he thinks she has, set her free but keep an eye on her." After all, I had a feeling her disrespect was rooted in her love for Thorn. I couldn't fault her for that. Although, if she didn't learn to back off and leave him alone, knowing we were bonded, then things would be hard for her.

He dipped his chin. "Yes, my queen."

As I stood by the door, I stared in through the silver bars to Patrice. No longer was she made up to perfection. Now she wore a tattered dress. Her messy hair hung limply around her dirt-caked face, and smudges of grime painted her body. But it was her glowing eyes that told me she was starving for blood. She hadn't had any in over two weeks. She was young for a vampire, which I'd learned meant she had to feed more regularly.

The door opened, and she flinched as I entered. Asher and Nate were at my back while Alex and Thorn stopped near the inside of the door, in case she got by the three of us first. I doubted it completely. There was no way I would allow it.

Stepping close to her, I looked down in disgust and unfiltered hate. "Who else was in on this?"

She laughed dryly. "No one."

"Patrice, one last chance. Who else was in on this?"

Her upper lip rose. "You're pathetic."

Bending, I gripped the knife I'd stored in my boot, lifted it, and sliced it across her neck. Her blood sprayed out, covering me. Her eyes widened, and she gagged on her own blood.

"Bag," I ordered. Someone dropped a blood bag into my waiting hand. I slapped it to her mouth, and she drank greedily. Her neck knitted back together. "Who else, Patrice?"

"Fuck you," she rasped.

In response, I threw the bagged blood on the dust-covered ground. She cried out, until I sliced her newly healed neck open again. That time, I waited. I let her suffer by carving her neck open over and over while it tried to heal.

"Bag," I clipped. Another was deposited in my hand. "Who else, Patrice?"

"Selma," she whispered.

Before she drank all the blood down, I took it from her and dropped it to the floor.

"No!" she cried.

I shook my head. "You shouldn't have been a part of it. You should have stayed well away from me. Instead, you took from me. You helped kill Ezra. For that, you will suffer." I turned and walked away, catching a guard's eyes. "Keep doing what I was. Until I say otherwise."

He bowed. Respect shone in his eyes. "Yes, my queen."

"And send someone after Selma. I want her down here."

"As you wish, my queen," another guard answered, and three of them peeled away from the wall outside Patrice's cell to do as I bid.

I would make a mockery of them and make sure no one wanted to deal with my wrath again while I was at it.

As I moved toward Barrett's cell, worry seeped into my mind. Already I'd hardened myself to a point where a part of my innocence withered away. There were vile creatures out there, even within these walls, and it was up to me to deal with them. I had to be strong; I had to build a steel fortress around my own emotions sometimes. What worried me the most about it, about this newer unbreakable side to me, was if my mates would despise seeing me like that and the queen I was becoming? Would they hate me? Would they find what I did disgusting? I could have had them handle this for me. They would have. They were used to fighting, killing, but I didn't want them to touch her. To have spoken with her. Did they understand why I had to deal with these vermin myself? I wanted to make them hurt, like I had the people I'd killed to feed, the ones with evil intent, and the ones Ezra had taught me to hunt.

Ezra. My chest speared with sorrow. I bit my bottom lip to stop the emotion taking hold.

Did my mates, the men who were made for me and me for them, understand I bloodied myself for Ezra? He had to be avenged, and I had to be the one to do it.

Would they think of me differently because of these events?

"Never, love," Asher answered quietly. "You are beautiful and amazing. No matter what side you show us, we will always want you." Lately, he and Thorn kept their emotions locked away from me since I'd already been feeling so much, but they opened themselves wide. Hope, love, pride, even arousal crawled over and inside of me from them.

"Thank you." I let my gratitude show in my voice. I doubted there would be a day I wouldn't feel lucky to have my mates. Yes, even Nate.

Another guard opened the cell door. Stepping through, I looked down at Barrett on his cot in the corner of the room. He was in the same shape as Patrice, but being a mage, he hungered for food and water instead. He sat up quickly and curled into himself.

"Leave me alone!" he cried. I glanced at his ankle. It still held the device that took away his magic.

I shook my head. "I can't. I won't. Ezra was mine, and you killed him. Where do you think that leaves you?"

"Y-You can't kill me. I was protecting the people from that beast."

Lies. I could scent it. "No one knew what he was. As far as people knew, he was a dog. And *mine*," I said, low and harsh. "Why did you kill him?"

He shook his head.

When I stepped closer, he shouted, "What did you do to Patrice?"

"You'll find out if you don't talk, because I'll do the same to you." I gestured down my body. "You see her blood. Do you want yours to join hers?"

He quivered. His scent shifted. Sweat and fear. He opened

his mouth and said quietly, "Since your family was safe, I tried to take matters into my own hands. The spell wouldn't work on your mates—"

"You tried?" I bellowed. My powers surged, my eyes glowed, my claws and teeth extended.

He whimpered and tried to scuttle back, but he was already in the corner. I enjoyed seeing and scenting his terror. He deserved it.

"They were safe. You were safe. I couldn't touch anyone but the mutt."

"Shit," I heard Alex curse behind me.

Facing Alex, I saw dread dipping his brows, darkening his eyes, slumping his shoulders. "What?" I asked.

He bowed his head, eyes to the floor. "It's my fault, my queen."

"Look at me," I ordered softly. He straightened. "What are you saying, Alex?"

I could tell he wanted to move his gaze away from me. Guilt flickered in his eyes, but his focus stayed on me when he said, "I layered a spell over us and you. I should have for Ezra, but I didn't think." His jaw clenched. "It's my fault he got to him."

"No," I stated, resolute. I took the steps to be in front of Alex and cupped his cheeks, staring into his agonized gaze. "It's not your fault. Never your fault. It's theirs. They wanted to hurt me, hurt all of my mates, but couldn't because *you* protected us."

"But I should have—"

"Don't take on that blame. *Please.* It's not your fault." Truth carried my words. I wouldn't blame Alex and didn't want him to blame himself either. I could only hope he heard the certainty in my voice. I would have shared it in my emotions with him, but we'd yet to finalize the bond. Something that would change and soon; I needed my mates. It would be safer for all of us to be connected completely. I wanted all them to know that even through my grief, they're mine, something I hadn't shown them since we'd lost Ezra. They needed to know I would protect them, I would love them, and I would kill for them.

It was Barrett, Odin, Patrice, and Selma's fault. They were all guilty for the event.

"Okay," he said on an exhale.

Smiling, I nodded. "Okay." Leaning up, I brushed my lips against his. His heart galloped from the first touch of my lips.

"Hellhounds should be able to repel magic thrown at them. Why didn't that happen?" Thorn interrupted; I was sure it was more to himself than everyone. However, it had me turning back to Barrett.

He shook his head. "I don't know how it worked. I don't."

Maybe Ezra was different from any other hellhound. It was all I could think of.

Brushing the thought away, for now, I moved back toward Barrett and called over my shoulder, "Asher."

"Yes, my queen?"

"I need you to help me with something because I have a feeling he won't tell the truth, no matter what I do."

Asher stepped to my side as we stopped in front of Barrett. "Make him tell me if he's romantically involved with Odin."

Barrett let out a noise and buried his head into his knees, crying over and over, "No."

I was glad when Asher's eyes bled to green, and his fangs dropped. Thankfully, my libido didn't kick into hyperdrive—

it certainly wasn't the time. The room chilled as his power thickened throughout.

Asher leaned forward a little. His voice was soft, almost lulling when he said, "Look at me."

Barrett shook his head repeatedly.

"Look at me," Asher's voice deepened.

Slowly, Barrett lifted his head and gazed into Asher's eyes. "Is Odin your lover?"

"Yes."

Asher sucked his power back in, and he returned to his human appearance as he moved back. Barrett blinked over and over, coming out of the trance Asher had put him in.

"I thought so," I said.

"What? You talk about changing things, and you're against me loving a man?"

I laughed humorlessly. "No. You have it wrong. I'm all about people loving whoever they want. But… you took someone *I* loved."

His eyes widened as understanding registered. He paled, and his heart beat erratically. "No." He gasped. "This is different. He was just a damn hellhound."

"Ezra was family!" I yelled, my hands balling into fists. Over my shoulder, I ordered, "Bring Odin in here."

"Please, no. Please don't do this. I love him."

"I love Ezra. If I'd begged, would you have dropped the spell? Would you have let me save him?"

His lips snapped closed.

Yeah, I didn't think so.

"Stop, unhand me," we heard shouted. "You can't do this to me. I have rights. I am an adviser."

I turned enough to see Odin being forced through the doorway by two guards. He looked in the same state as his lover. His ankles and hands were chained together. Only he still held a note of stubbornness, or arrogance and distaste. His face screwed up at the sight of me. "What's the meaning of this?"

With speed behind me, I swiftly moved behind Odin, gripped his head, and using my queen strength, I ripped it from his shoulders. More blood sprayed out, coating me. Barrett started screaming when Odin's body fell to the floor. I threw Odin's head over near Barrett.

"A life for a life," I called loudly. Barrett keened and rocked on his bed. I didn't sense any repulsion from Asher or Thorn. I even glanced to Alex and Nate, but to my shock, they showed understanding. Nate nodded.

"My queen," someone said.

Turning, I saw Felnick standing in the doorway. "Yes?" I asked.

"You have a call. It's important."

"Now?"

"Yes, my queen."

"Who is it?" Thorn asked.

"Lucifer."

What the fuckety-fuck?

CHAPTER TWO
PAIGE

We strode to the meeting room where I would take a call from Lucifer. "Are you sure it's the devil himself?" I asked again.

Felnick nodded. "Yes, my queen."

"As in *The* Prince of Darkness?" I queried and wondered if this was an actual dream. Then I glanced down at myself and saw the blood coating my hands, body, and probably face. It couldn't be a dream. *Dammit.*

"Yes, my queen," Felnick answered.

I glanced at Asher beside me. "What would he want with me?"

"I'm unsure, love."

Then to Thorn, I asked, "Was the former queen acquainted with him?"

Him.

The devil.

Lucifer.

I still couldn't wrap my head around the fact the devil was on the phone waiting for me. It was another moment where, if I still peed, I would be filling my leather pants about now.

"I had heard she'd spoken with him on a few occasions," Thorn said.

Laughter bubbled up, but I clamped my lips together to stop it from exploding. The former queen spoke with the devil on a few occasions.

The devil was real.

Hell was real… I guessed.

Of course it was all real, or else Lucifer wouldn't be waiting on the phone for me. But how did they get reception down there?

My mind and world had been blown wide open, and I wasn't sure I was ready for more things like this. Although, at least it would keep my mind off the gaping hole in my chest over losing Ezra for a while.

We entered my office—it had been the former queen's, but I'd taken it over just last week. Yasmin had been in and decorated it to what she thought I would like. She hadn't done too bad, except for the painting of, well, to me, it looked like two dogs going at it, but she swore it was some abstract art piece.

I made my way around the desk, and with a shaky hand, I picked up the phone and placed it against my ear. When I nodded at Felnick, he pressed the button.

Shit. How was I supposed to greet the Prince of Darkness?

A cool hand touched the back of my neck, and calmness spread through me. I glanced at Asher with an appreciative smile. "Paige Alice speaking."

"Ah, Paige Alice, the new ghoul queen. It's a pleasure to hear your voice." His voice was smooth and soft, almost like a purr in my ear.

"I'm presuming this is… Lucifer?"

"You presume right, my dear." I could hear the humor in his voice.

"What can I do for you, Lucifer?" My lips twitched. Either this was some elaborate prank, or I was actually speaking with the devil.

"It's what I can do for you, my dear."

"And that would be?"

"It's not something to speak of over the phone. I shall be in your area in a couple of weeks. Please prepare some rooms for me and a few of my people."

I dipped my brows in confusion and pressed my lips together in annoyance. "You could have passed this message on to my guard Felnick. I was in the middle of something." I gasped at my own words. Did people talk to Satan like that? Would he smite me and send me to burn in Hell for the rest of my existence?

Lucifer snorted. "And what could have been so important that you would have missed *my* call?"

"Ripping someone's head off because he and his lover took someone from me." My voice darkened toward the end. "No one kills someone I love."

When laughter sounded on the other end, I wanted to slide my hand through the receiver and tear out his vocal cords. Instead, I hung the damn phone up with a slam.

My heart beat frantically, already worried, and that was even before my brain could register what I'd just done.

"You hung up on Lucifer," Alex croaked while pointing at the phone.

My hand shook as I ran it over my face, probably smearing blood everywhere. I shrugged off Asher's hand and placed both hands to the desk, leaning into it. What did I do? He could come here and kill us all, probably with a thought. Fear churned my stomach. Fear for everyone around me, not myself.

"My queen, would you like me to call him back and beg forgiveness?" Felnick offered. His whole body trembled.

"No," I said, yet I was unsure. After a moment's consideration, I voiced my thoughts. "I can't show weakness. He may be Lucifer, but he needs to know I won't be messed with." I glanced at my men. Alex seemed worried by the way he chewed on his bottom lip. Nate looked bored. It was Asher's and Thorn's smiles that eased the anguish in my belly.

I straightened and then jolted when my phone rang again. I waited a couple of beats before I answered it on speakerphone. "Paige Alice."

"Do you know no one has hung up on me before?" His voice was hard and cold. Eerily so.

"First time for everything," I blurted.

Lucifer hummed under his breath. "I think I like you, Paige Alice. Very much so."

The men, all except Felnick, grumbled or growled low. But my ears also picked up another snarl from the phone, then Lucifer cursed before he said, "I shall contact you before we arrive, Paige."

"How many should we expect?" I asked.

"Six."

"Very well."

"Until then," he replied with a smile in his voice, and then I got dial tone.

I ended the call and glanced around. Asher, Thorn, and Nate now all wore frowns. Felnick looked nervous by the way he shuffled from one foot to the other. Only Alex offered me a soft smile since the situation was over.

"I don't fucking like this," Nate announced gruffly.

"Me neither," Asher said.

"At least he sounded okay after Paige hung up on him," Alex offered. I gave him a grin. He was always quick to see the best in situations to ease my fears, even when worried. I loved him for it.

Nate shook his head. "It's Lucifer. He shouldn't have been okay with it."

Thorn nodded. "He's up to something."

"But what?" Asher put in. The room fell silent.

"Maybe I should call him back and tell him not to come," I thought aloud.

Felnick whimpered. I knew he was a hardass, since he was one who'd fought and killed to protect my family, yet it seemed when it came to the devil, he wanted to meld with the floor.

He shook his head again and again. "Not unless we want to die."

"He handled my hanging up on him well. I'm sure he'd be okay with me telling him he's not welcome."

"Question is, do we need to know what he wants to say?" Nate said.

I bit my bottom lip as I thought about it. Whatever he wanted to tell me couldn't be said over the phone. But if Lucifer came here, I was more worried about my men and people. Yet, if I did tell him no, it could mean we'd be worse off.

Groaning, I slapped the desk. "He'll have to come, and whatever he has to say or do, we'll need to be ready," I said.

Nate snorted. "There's no getting ready for Lucifer. He could kill with a blink of his eyes."

"I meant the castle." I hadn't, but it made me sound like I knew what I was saying. Ignoring Nate's obnoxious snort, I glanced at Felnick. "Speak with Gregory. Let him, and only him for now, know who will be coming and how many he's bringing with him."

He bowed, saying, "Yes, my queen." Then he rushed out the door, closing it behind him.

"Have any of you dealt with Lucifer before?"

"Never," Thorn said.

Alex shook his head.

Asher glanced at Nate, who sighed. "Neither of us have met him personally, but we've heard stories about him."

"Like what?" I asked, pulling out the chair at my desk and sitting in it. Alex took a chair opposite me. Nate leaned against the wall, crossing his arms over his chest. When Thorn sat on the corner of my desk, my eyes didn't stray from his butt... only it wasn't the time to admire or want to see it naked. Asher moved around my desk and sat in the chair beside Alex. His knowing look said I'd been caught checking out Thorn. Even Alex was blushing and smiling slightly. Nate rolled his eyes at me, but I caught his lips twitching. However, he thinned them and gave me a pointed look.

Right. It wasn't the time.

Just as my eyes strayed toward Thorn's rump, Nate sighed. I swung my gaze back to him as he started speaking. "We've heard tales of Lucifer never wanting to venture far from the underworld, yet he's willing to because he wants to meet you. We know he's a hard ruler, but like in all domains, people like to test things. He's ruthless, a womanizer, and you wouldn't want to be on his bad side."

Asher added, "He's feared by many. Even the council."

"Do you think he was the one who sent the demons after me in the first place?"

Thorn shook his head. "We can't be certain, but it's something we need to consider, especially with him coming here."

His cell phone rang. He quickly answered while I asked, "But wouldn't he have authority over all of them? So, it has to be him."

"There are millions of demons," Asher said, and I shuddered at the thought, "and being so many, there are ones who will do as they please. Lucifer is one man, after all. He can't keep an eye on everything. Demons are corrupt beings; they would do anything to gain power. So many seek more power to try and overthrow Lucifer."

"It would be good to believe Satan can be an ally," Alex murmured.

"There's nothing we can do about it now," Thorn said, ending the call he'd been on. "All we can do is wait. We have other matters to deal with for now."

I hated when he was right. "Selma. No one's found her yet?"

Thorn shook his head, his lips pressing into a thin line of worry. "That call was from my brethren. Unfortunately, she's disappeared."

"But can they tell if she's left the community altogether?" I asked.

His brows dipped, and I already knew it was more bad news. "They followed her trail. She's out of our area."

Dammit. I wanted a different answer.

Selma, a vampire who looked all of sixteen but was probably thousands of years old, had been on the Barrett-Odin bandwagon and, like them, hadn't wanted change to happen within the community. Somehow she'd escaped. Perhaps she'd been smart enough to know they would give her up, so she'd gone into hiding before I could get my hands on her. I had no doubt her involvement meant she played a big part in the attack on Ezra.

And all because they didn't want people to love who they wanted and, of course, they didn't approve that my mates were not of my own kind. They looked down on shifters especially, thought of them as lowly beings. It came as no surprise that they despised me making a shifter my adviser or how I intended to let different races work together.

They were old, I was new, and the change had to happen.

I wasn't the only one who thought my decision would be for the better.

Alma, the former queen's seer, and now mine, had seen how my bringing in these changes would better our community. I believed it also.

Of course, not a day went by that I didn't freak out about being thrust into the role of queen.

Even right then I felt like a fraud.

I would have given so much to be back in my small apartment with Ezra at my side. I'd work, see my family, hunt… all with Ezra.

But then I wouldn't have my men.

I wouldn't have bossy and scary Asher, my vampire. Angry and annoying Nate, my shifter. Sweet and smart Alex, my mage. Cunning and fierce Thorn, my ghoul.

My life wouldn't have been complete without them in it.

Even when loss still stung me.

Love rolled over me, causing my fears and worries to recede inside me. I glanced up to Thorn as he stood from the desk and walked my way. When I scooted my chair back, he took my hand and dragged me up, wrapping his arms around my shoulders.

"Things will get easier," he promised.

Hands touched my waist, and a chest pressed into my back. Asher. "Eventually, you'll be too bored with nothing happening."

Resting my head on Thorn's shoulder, I shook it. "I doubt I could ever be bored." I couldn't ever be, not when I had my mates. They grounded me. I glanced at my glowering Nate and to my softly smiling Alex.

"She gets into too much trouble for things to be easy," Nate commented.

I shot him the middle finger.

CHAPTER THREE
THORN

It had been a few days since we'd found out Lucifer would be paying us a visit, and in that time, Paige's moods had been depleting. My gaze didn't stray from her as she sat reading on the couch with papers scattered around her. They were appeals from the people in the community. I'd told her we could all go through them, but she'd said she needed a distraction.

I understood she'd cared for her hellhound deeply, but I hadn't understood how strong their connection had been. Even though she had her emotions locked, there was still a tiny amount of heartache that seeped through. I hated to see her sad, but there wasn't a thing I could do. Maybe Asher and I had been right when we'd discussed Ezra being more than just a hellhound. The way he'd been with Paige was different from any other hellhound we'd previously encountered. Usually they were crazed beasts doing their master's bidding by destroying or killing. Ezra had expressions, had character, and I was pretty damn sure he'd had a soul.

He'd been different.

I glanced over Paige's head to see Asher at the desk going through his own work, but his attention was on Paige. He was worried about her as much as I was.

There was an abrupt knock on the door before it opened and Nate strode in, leaving the door ajar for two women—one a ghoul, the other human—and a shifter male to roll in trays of refreshments. Alex entered after them. Paige looked up as they bowed. "My queen."

She offered them a smile that didn't reach her eyes. She saved those for us when we were all alone, but it also seemed we were the only ones who got her to fully smile, as well as her family.

"Thank you," she said.

Asher stood and came around the desk. It was bad timing because he got close to one of the women and she smiled up at him with adoration while moving around the cart and happened to brush against him.

Power filled the room. I snapped my eyes to Paige as she jumped up, crouching on the couch. Her eyes changed, her claws grew, and a snarl dripped from between her lips. "Mine."

Her hands went to the back of the couch, and I could read her purpose—she was about to attack the woman. I flew out of my chair just as Nate raced at Paige. We circled her, holding her, yet with her power, she managed to take a few steps toward the screaming woman.

"Alex, get them out," Nate yelled. Alex's eyes bled to purple, and more power filled the room. A bubble popped up around the women and man, and slowly they floated out of the room. Asher flashed in front of Paige while Alex followed the floating people out.

"Clear their minds," Nate called.

"I know," Alex snapped.

Asher took the struggling Paige's face in his hands and forced her gaze to latch on to his glowing green vampire eyes.

"Paige, my love. Focus on me." His voice threaded softly through the room. He ignored her growls and leaned in to press his lips against the corner of her mouth but moved back quickly to avoid her sharp teeth.

"She needs to feed," I told them.

"She was about to eat," Nate said.

"No. She needs flesh. Fucking hell, I should have known earlier."

"Not your fault. Too much has been happening," Asher said.

"We need to clear her mind enough to get her into the kitchens," I ordered.

"Why can't we just call up for food?" Nate asked.

Asher shook his head. "It's the easy way out. She will hate what's happened, even feel weak and worthless for it. She needs to see how strong she can be. All she needs is a distraction to bring her back to us." With that said, he stuck his hand into her pants. Her growls paused. She hissed and then froze. Slowly her power eased, her claws retracting, as did her teeth. Lastly, her eyes swirled back to dark blue.

Nate snorted. He released his hold to cross his arms over his chest and seemed annoyed, but I noticed his eyes hadn't moved away from Asher's fingers teasing her under her clothes.

"Asher," she moaned.

"There you are, my love." He withdrew his fingers. She whimpered in protest before her face burned with the realization of her actions.

"I would have killed her," she whispered.

"Let's get you some food," I said and started to lead her to the door. When I glanced back, I caught Asher licking his fingers. Nate watched him, his eyes darker than usual.

"We'll catch up," Asher said. "I'm hungry myself, and Alex should be in soon."

The door opened and Alex stepped through. Paige wasn't fully with it, or she would have wanted to stay around to watch Asher feed. However, she kept my pace to the door, mumbling about being the worst queen ever.

Alex looked at us with concern. "I've got her," I reassured him. "Meet us in the kitchens."

He gave me a sad smile and nodded. As he started to shut the door after us, I heard, "You feed off me," Nate stated. "Not him today."

My lips tipped up. Nate was certainly more possessive of Alex since his wolf had claimed him—something Paige didn't know about yet. But Asher and I could read the signs clearly the day after it had happened.

I curled my arm tighter around Paige's waist as we made our way down the stairs. She grumbled under her breath some more.

"It's not your fault, Paige," I whispered into her ear.

She huffed. "I would have killed her, Thorn."

"We had you, sweetheart."

She nodded. Yet, since she'd opened her emotions probably unintentionally from her hunger, I could still feel her disgust and fear.

"We just need to make sure you feed more regularly." If anything, I felt guilty for not seeing it sooner. Our queen was starved, but she hadn't realized it.

"Just… hold me tighter. I wish the others had come as well."

"You don't trust I can handle you?" I teased, not letting my pride be wounded as I knew she was still scared.

"That's not it—"

I kissed her temple. "I know, sweetheart," I told her as we entered the deserted kitchens. The thing was, I knew she would hold herself together because of her people that lingered in the halls as we made our way to the kitchens. She hungered, but she forced it down, knowing her pains would settle shortly. "See, you made it. You're strong, Paige."

She laughed without humor. "If Asher hadn't stuck his hand in my pants, I would still be a growling psycho ready to kill things."

"Yet, you pulled it back in, walked out of there, made it downstairs and into the kitchens while people moved around, and kept your hunger from surfacing again. Sit here, sweetheart." I pulled out a chair at the counter and kissed her neck. "The hunger didn't win. You did. If she hadn't have gotten close to Asher, nothing would have happened."

She watched me as I headed to the walk-in meat refrigerator, that contained the freshest meals, beside the huge freezer and asked, "I thought my possessiveness would settle once the bond was completed."

I paused outside the door and glanced back. "I think it had something to do with being hungry and stressed, sweetheart."

"I'll need to be on top of it then since my new job is very stressful."

"That, and I'm sure your mates can help you stress less." I winked and opened the door, but I didn't miss the smile, a real one, coming over Paige. I loved seeing her smile, especially when I felt her love shining through the devastation and worry. I grabbed some meat off the hook and took it back out to Paige, glad to see her still in a lighter mood. I hoped, with the help of some food, she might get some sleep.

As I cut off some human flesh and placed it in bowls, I asked, "How's Eric liking his job?"

She laughed, her eyes never straying from the bowl. "I never knew how much of a nerd he is. He's having the time of his life taking over the role of investment manager." She grinned warmly. "Thank you for helping him find it."

"My pleasure," I said, pushing the bowl and fork her way. On the first mouthful, she moaned in the back of her throat, and my cock thickened. To distract myself, I took my own forkful, only I should have looked away from Paige to be distracted because she was too seductive. Her eyes had fluttered closed. She licked her lips after each bite, and she moved around in her seat like she was riding a dick.

My cock throbbed. I'd wanted to be inside her since the last time. Even a couple of times a day, but after everything that had happened, I hadn't made a move in that area. She'd been grieving, and I would have been the biggest jerk if I'd started something.

Closing my eyes, I clenched my jaw and scolded myself. My poor mate was starving, and all I could do was think about sliding into her. How wet, soft, tight and inviting she would be.

"Thorn," Paige called softly. I opened my eyes to her. "Would it be wrong if you fucked me on the countertop where people made their meals?"

My fork clattered to the floor, and just as I made a move around the bench, the door to the kitchen opened. Michael and his very pregnant wife, Leona, walked in, laughing about something. They froze and slammed their mouths closed when they spotted us.

All desire in the room fell away.

"It's all right. Come in," I offered with a smile and a wave.

Paige shoved the last of the meat into her mouth, making her look like a chipmunk with how big her cheeks were as she chewed wildly while the couple slowly made their way over to us.

Was she ashamed of what she was or just what she ate?

It was something I would ask when it was just the two of us. Then I'd reassure her it was natural and no one in our community cared. If they did, they wouldn't have followed the former queen in the first place.

I moved in beside Paige and wound an arm around her waist. She shivered at my touch, which caused me to smile.

Once they were close enough, they bowed, Michael helping his wife bend. "My queen," they said together. Paige shook her head and stepped up to them. She reached out and assisted Leona to stand. Only the woman was so shocked by it she gasped, her knees wobbled, and Michael had to pick her up in his arms.

Paige rushed over and grabbed a chair. "Here, sit her here."

Michael helped Leona into it, but all Leona could do was stare up at Paige in awe. Paige smiled down at her, asking, "How's everything going?"

Leona opened her mouth, then snapped it closed before she made a noise. Michael chuckled while I watched on with a grin. Finally, Michael came to his wife's rescue and said, "We must thank you again, Your Majesty, for the doctor and for allowing us to stay within the castle walls."

"It's not a problem. I like to have my advisers close, so thank you for moving in."

Leona cleared her throat, then whispered, "It's been many, many decades since shifters were seen as more than dirt under *others'* shoes. There's never enough thank-yous we could give for the things you've done."

Paige shrugged. "I can't understand how that happened,

why shifters were seen as lesser beings to the rest of the supernatural community. But I'm glad I can be a part of helping others to see shifters are important as well. Even if it's within these walls."

"For now," I added.

Paige smiled over at me before glancing back down at Leona. Paige's hand fluttered out toward the horse shifter. "Is everything all right with the baby?"

Paige's features softened even more. I'd seen her with her niece and nephew, she loved children, and it had me wondering if there would ever be a time or a way she could eventually have her own. As far as I knew, even with her queen power, she'd be unable to get pregnant. The knowledge saddened me because she would be a great mother.

However, the former queen had only ever been with her own species, and ghouls were infertile, much like vampires. But our queen, our mate, had a shifter and a mage whose bodies were alive. Could it happen then? I enjoyed the thought of Paige pregnant too much. We were her family; we all would care for any child as our own, no matter its race. It was something I needed to find out.

"Yes, she's happy and healthy. Ready to see the world any day now," Michael said proudly. Leona smiled up at him warmly while rubbing her belly. "We came down for a snack since it seems Little Miss is in need of chocolate cake."

Paige laughed lightly. "Chocolate cake sounds good to me."

"I'll see if I can find any," I told her.

"Thank you," she replied. Just as she was about to look my way, Leona took her hand. Paige's gaze snapped back down to her as Leona placed their hands over her belly. Paige melted. I'd never seen that look on her face or the one where it brightened blissfully as she giggled out, "She kicked."

Yes, I had to find out if our queen could have children. I knew it wasn't the time for it yet, but I prayed that things would eventually settle.

CHAPTER FOUR
ASHER

"You feed off me. Not him today," Nate stated as the door to the office closed after Thorn took Paige out. I knew Thorn would be able to help Paige in the way she needed. There would also be guards following their every move, so I stayed back and arched my brow at Nate.

"Nate," Alex scolded. "I can help Asher out."

"No," he snarled. He strode right up to me, tilted his head to the side, and ordered, "Fucking eat." I glanced over at Alex, who looked irritated, his nostrils flaring, yet his eyes told me he found the protectiveness sweet.

I glanced back down to Nate's neck, the pulse ticking away under the skin. He'd never offered me his blood before. Was he only doing it now so I wouldn't get close to Alex? Had his wolf truly claimed Alex as a mate?

"We should talk about this."

He grabbed my arms, tugged me closer, and barked, "Another day. Just eat and hurry the fuck up before—"

My fangs dropped just before I embedded them into Nate's neck. On the first pull of his blood, as it touched my tongue, I moaned around the rich, earthy, yet tangy taste. Nate held me tighter, and his warm breath fanned over my shoulder and onto my skin where my shirt folded open. When his hands dropped to my hips, I placed a hand on the opposite side of Nate's neck and the other at his waist, dragging him close so he was flush against me. Nate's wolf woke, and he growled. His hands on my hips squeezed painfully. The wolf was uncertain about me taking his blood, and his damn mouth was close to my throat; he could easily rip it out. I needed to stop feeding, but I enjoyed his taste too much. Just like it had been hard for me to stop feeding from Alex for the first time.

Another growl rumbled out of him. I opened my eyes as they bled to green and saw Alex stepping up behind Nate.

"It's all right. You're all right," he cooed into Nate's shoulder, the same side as I drank from so our eyes held each other's. I felt Alex's hands on Nate's sides as they ran up and down gently, softly, reassuringly. "You're fine," he whispered and kissed Nate's shoulder.

Since I held Nate close, I felt the first stir of his cock thickening.

Christ.

My own dick responded. After another hard pull of his blood, where I savored his taste, I withdrew my fangs and straightened. Stepping back, I watched as Nate lifted his head. His nostrils flared. A moment later, he gripped Alex's hand at his side and dragged it around to his front, then down to run over his length behind his jeans.

Fuck.

I'd been with many men and women. Though, it had been many years since I'd desired for two men together. Until then. Witnessing Nate's dark gaze and Alex's heated one had me wanting to see them naked together. Where I may even join in on the fun. I hadn't been turned on in so long, except for the first night with Paige. She could draw my cock hard in an instant. It seemed watching my two brothers-in-arms touch each other could also have my cock rock-hard as well.

Never would I have thought I'd see this or feel it.

"Leave, Asher," Nate bit out.

"No," I clipped back quickly just as Alex undid the button to Nate's jeans and slowly lowered his zip.

Then the door burst open, and in it stood Gregory, blood dripping from his forehead. "Help, please."

Nate did his jeans up, and we all faced Gregory. "What happened?" I demanded.

He stumbled in. "Please, come with me. Help. Please."

Alex was the first to move toward him. "Tell us on the way," he said. Gregory nodded. He was out the door, running in seconds. Alex followed. I glanced at Nate, whose jaw was clenched before he took off after his claimed mate. I raced after them.

Nate and I caught up easily and heard, "The pack found us. He was going to leave for me, come here, but they won't let him. He got me away before they got him."

"Who?"

"My mate. My love. Jessup."

Nate stumbled. "Jessup? But he's the alpha of the wolf pack. He has a mate. They have that fuckhead of a son. How is he your mate?"

Gregory shook his head. "The woman is the female alpha who joined with Jessup, but they aren't mates. Hers died. Jessup's brother. They came together to conceive, and that was it. He's mine. I'm his. No one knew until now. I messed up…. I shouldn't have gone there and pushed him; they don't accept it. They'll kill him."

When we'd first arrived, we'd had an altercation with the local wolf pack. Nate had accepted the challenge to fight Fenris, Jessup's son, to claim Paige. If he hadn't, Fenris was willing to fight anyone to prove he had the strength to stand at Paige's side and rule the people.

He was a bad seed, and Nate had even told me Fenris's own parents warned that if Fenris won, it wouldn't be good. So it wasn't hard to guess who would be behind the attack on the alpha when they found him with a man for a mate.

"You might have to move up the challenge," I told Nate.

"With fucking pleasure, but I'm not becoming their alpha," he replied as we ran by the kitchens. Paige stepped out. "Fuck," Nate cursed.

"What's going on?" she called, her eyes wide in alarm.

"Keep going. I'll be there shortly," I informed Nate. I wound back to Paige and Thorn. Four guards stood back from them. "Jessup, the wolf alpha, is in trouble. We're—"

"Let's go," Paige said and took off after Nate and the others.

"Christ," I clipped. "Stay close to her," I ordered the guards, and they followed Paige quickly. I looked at Thorn. "Nate may have to challenge Fenris early. If she's there for it…"

"It could be a shitstorm," he finished. We both rushed out the doors. The people who were still awake watched as we flew by them. "Is Alex there? He might be able to put her in a bubble like before," Thorn suggested.

I nodded. "It's an idea." And probably the best one, because if the challenge went ahead and Paige saw Nate in trouble, she could break all the laws of the challenge and probably break a few extra bones along the way. "Although, we may have to watch Alex too."

Understanding dawned on Thorn's face. "That's true. Let's see how it goes. I might call in more guards."

"Could be good."

Thorn and I stopped behind Paige in the woods just as she asked, "Gregory, what are you doing here?" She gasped when he faced her. "You're bleeding? Why are you bleeding? Who do I need to hurt? *No one* makes you bleed. You feed me, take care of us, make our beds."

Jesus. The things that came out of her mouth could have me bursting with laughter, but it wasn't the moment to do so.

"I'm fine, my queen, but it's Jessup who is not."

"How? Why? And how do you know?"

Gregory glanced from Alex to Nate and then me. I shook my head and said, "She doesn't know yet."

He bowed his head and met Paige's gaze. "I've only recently discovered Jessup is my mate. The pack as a whole doesn't know. But a few have discovered the truth, and a few don't approve. He wanted to keep me safe until he could change things…. N-Now they're making him pay for being with a man. He got me away, but he needs help."

Paige opened her mouth, but Nate spoke first. "Jessup isn't mated to the woman. They're the alpha couple, but she was mated to his brother. They only came together to have a kid."

Paige nodded, then clapped her hands and said, "Right, let's go save Jessup and kick some bigotry ass while we're at it." She started forward until Alex grabbed her arm gently.

She glanced at him, and he told her, "I'm sorry, Paige. I do enjoy seeing you kick ass"—a few of the guards chuckled —"but Nate will have to take point on this mission. It's a wolf pack we're dealing with, and Nate being, well, a wolf, he'll be better at sorting it."

She nodded and curled her arms around Alex's waist. Of course, he blushed, gazing down at her like she was the treasured prize she was. "You're right." She stepped back and took his hand. "I'll hold myself back."

Nate snorted. "I'll believe it when I see it."

She glared over at him. "You say shit like that and I won't." She glanced at her guards. "Sorry, I'm not acting very queen-like."

They bowed, and one said, "You be whomever you wish when you want, and we will follow you, my queen."

Tenderness bloomed inside of her and shone out. I knew Thorn would be feeling the same. "Thank you." She smiled.

"Please, my queen, may we move forward?" Gregory asked. Fear had his body twitching.

"Of course. Lead the way, Nate."

Nate grunted and took point. I followed behind him to his left and Thorn to his right. Gregory stepped up behind us, then Paige and Alex, swinging their joined hands. After them, the guards joined the line. Only one had his eyes on my mate's ass. When I let out a hiss, all eyes shot to me, and when the guard saw I was directing my glowing eyes on him, he blanched. There was his one chance. If I caught him ogling her again, I would make him pay in pain. He nodded as if reading my thoughts. Good.

Turning back around, we rushed through another couple of miles before we stepped into a clearing that held at least thirty cabins scattered here and there. I hadn't understood why the wolf shifters kept to themselves in this area when all the other shifters lived in the village behind the castle. That was until Thorn had explained that the former queen allowed the wolves their own area because of their large group, as long as they swore their allegiance to her.

Passing a few cabins, we entered the open space where we found Jessup strung up by his arms to a pole in the middle.

Gregory cried out. He made a run for Jessup, but Paige grabbed him and held him close. "Not yet," she said. "It's all right," she added, patting his back.

Upon Gregory's cry, Jessup slowly pulled his head up. There wasn't a part of his face that didn't look cracked, bruised, or bloodied.

He was alpha, the strongest of them all… how had this happened?

My answer came when five shifters, in their human form, stepped out from between the cabins. The one at the front was Fenris.

"You dare come onto pack land without an invite?" Fenris snarled, his upper lip raised.

Nate stepped forward. "We had concerns for the alpha. We came to help. No invitation needed."

"I'm alpha now." His gaze flicked to Paige, and he licked his lips. "And soon to be king by your side. We'll rule well together."

Paige opened her mouth to respond, but I caught Alex tightening his hold on her waist and she snapped her mouth closed. Instead, she just glared Fenris's way.

"Do not fucking look at her," Nate growled.

Fenris tensed. "Do not fucking come on my lands and talk to me that way. I'm alpha here. I'll deal with you in the challenge."

"How did you become alpha?" Nate nodded to Jessup, who's head had dropped back down, but his eyes stayed half open and on the ground while he listened. "Jessup isn't dead, or did he step down?" Nate questioned.

Fenris spat to the side. "He's filth. He's no alpha."

"So he stepped down?"

Fenris's jaw clenched.

"They were going to kill him in the morning" came a voice. The alpha female stepped out.

"Mom, get the fuck inside," Fenris clipped.

"Don't you 'Mom' me, boy. You disgrace our ways. You do this to your father—"

"He's no father of mine," he roared.

She shook her head. "You disappoint me. Disappoint the pack. There was no fair fight. You all took Jessup to the ground when you caught him and beat him senseless, then strung him up to make anyone too scared to go against you and your ways." Her eyes moved to Paige. "Times are changing."

"Not in this pack," Fenris yelled. "Fine, you want a fair fight? Release him and I'll rip his throat out."

She laughed humorlessly. "You would fight a man in his condition? Pathetic."

"Have care, Mother," he warned. Other shifters, some in their wolf form, some human, emerged from inside the cabins.

"Or what? You'll fight me? You'll beat me? Because you want power, you want to be alpha and have the pack fear you instead of leading it with love, happiness, and an iron fist? When has Jessup steered the pack wrong? He hasn't been challenged in decades."

"He steers us wrong by fucking that piece of shit over there," he screamed. "He's not pack. He's not wolf. Not even a fucking shifter."

The alpha woman shook her head. Fenris glared at the obvious disappointment in her eyes. "Times are changing. We need to keep up with them."

"We don't and we won't." Fenris threw out a hand toward Jessup. "Take him down. We fight for the alpha position."

Nate took another step forward. "On behalf of Jessup

Falk, I'll fight for his right as alpha. I'll also be completing the challenge, set for the full moon in a couple of days, tonight."

"No!" Paige cried out just as Fenris smiled wickedly.

"Accepted." Fenris laughed.

CHAPTER FIVE
PAIGE

Panic gripped my chest. I started forward but was grabbed quickly. I fought their hold, not even knowing who held me. All I could see was Nate stepping closer into the circle as he removed his T-shirt. "Nate, no, you can't do this," I told him, my throat thick with tension.

"Paige, stop. He has to," Thorn said into my ear.

"No, he doesn't." I shook my head again and again. "No, I won't allow it."

Fenris let out a belly laugh. "Hear that, mutt? She won't allow it. You gonna stop to please your pussy?"

"Shut the fuck up. We doing this or not?"

"Not," I yelled. They ignored me.

Nate nodded, and I wanted to reach out to him to smack him upside the head or pick him up and run for the hills to protect him. I knew I couldn't, and I hated it. Wolves were proud creatures who lived by their own set of rules. If I interfered, it could mean bad things for not only us, but Jessup, Gregory, and Jessup's pack. I had to think about others rather than just me and my feelings. Still, knowing Nate was about to fight and could possibly be hurt, killed me inside. I gripped Thorn's arms around my waist and whimpered.

"He'll be fine," he whispered.

"He's strong," Alex said quietly from our side. Even though he was trying to reassure me, Alex looked like he'd swallowed something foul. He disliked what was about to happen as much as I did. I took his hand in mine again and brought it up to hold it against my chest.

"Skin or fur? I'll let you pick since I'll kill you in either form." Fenris grinned evilly.

"Skin," Nate replied. "But if the shift comes over either of us, there won't be any repercussions."

"Agreed," Fenris answered, then charged Nate, who braced.

Fenris hit Nate in the face so hard Nate's head whipped to the side. I slapped a hand over my mouth to keep the scream building at bay, not wanting to distract him. Alex's hand in mine squeezed harder, while Thorn held me tighter. Out of the corner of my eye, I saw Asher step up to Alex and place his hand on his shoulder. To my surprise, Nate grinned, only it wasn't a nice one. Fenris's cocky smile disappeared when Nate slowly turned his head back to face him.

Fenris went to hit him again, but Nate grabbed Fenris's fist in one hand and used the other to punch him in the gut. Fenris stumbled back, barely catching himself from falling, and snarled at Nate. Fenris bounced from one foot to another, his hand cocked in front of him like some type of boxer. Using his fingers, he called Nate forward, only Nate didn't move. He stood there and crossed his arms over his chest.

"Fight," Fenris roared.

Nate raised a brow.

"Fight me," Fenris yelled.

Nate relaxed his arms at his sides and took a step forward. Fenris charged again, jabbing his fist to the left, but Nate gracefully moved back. Fenris jabbed to the right, and Nate twirled out of the way.

I wanted to race in there, grab Nate's shoulders, and shake

the shit out of him. He needed to end this fight before my nerves ate at my beating organ.

Fenris swept out his leg, kicking Nate in the thigh before bouncing back. He spun back in, grabbed Nate on the back of the neck, and kneed him in the stomach before moving out of reach. Another smile splayed across Fenris's face. He was sure of himself now that he'd gotten a couple of shots in.

"Nate, stop dragging this out," Asher called.

Fenris's smile vanished. He straightened, glancing from Asher to Nate. It was then Nate snapped out his leg, kicking Fenris in the chest, sending him flying backward and landing with a thud on the ground. Growling low, he rolled onto all fours and, still in human form, charged Nate.

Nate braced again, and as soon as Fenris was close, Nate jumped, flipping in the air and landing on Fenris's back. His knees dug into Fenris's spine, his arm locking around Fenris's neck, squeezing. Fenris dropped to the ground, skidding along the dirt, scraping his skin, which would heal easily.

"Do you yield?" Nate offered, his voice rough and thick.

"No," Fenris rasped. He rolled, flipping Nate off, and jumped to his feet as Nate did. With a nod, two other shifters stepped up behind Nate and grabbed his arms.

"Foul play," I yelled. Dropping Alex's hand, I forced Thorn's arms off me and started toward them, ready to help.

In seconds, the coward Fenris punched, kicked, and then extended his claws, slashing at Nate's chest and stomach.

"Paige," Alex clipped in a vicious tone, one I hadn't heard from him, so it had me looking back. "I have this," he told me. His jaw clenched, his eyes glowed purple, and his hands and mouth moved. My clit pulsed, but I told it to get lost. I glanced back to Nate in time to see the shifters holding him stiffen.

Their arms fell away. Fenris cursed them but realized something was happening when their eyes widened. They let out a howl of pain right before we all heard their spines snapping in two and they tumbled to the ground.

Holy shit.

Nate lifted his head as his chest rose and fell rapidly. He was bloody and sore, but the smart-ass prick winked at me before shifting his gaze to Alex. I turned, and I'd never seen Alex look so scary before. His pulsating power had his hair sticking up everywhere, swaying in the invisible breeze only around him. His body was tense, his hands fisted at his sides, and his eyes were glowing brighter. He nodded once at Nate. I didn't catch what Nate did, but it had Alex relaxing, his power subsiding.

A harsh snarl had me facing Nate again. He'd shifted to his wolf form. His jeans shredded, falling to the floor. Fenris followed and changed into his wolf. Where Nate was a dark brown, Fenris was a light amber color.

They circled each other, growling. Fenris jumped forward, nipping at Nate, but Nate was too fast and bounced back, only to jump forward and snap his jaw at Fenris's side. Fenris let out a scared noise and tumbled back, popping back up onto his paws. They circled each other again, snarling.

Other wolves around the circle scraped with claws into the dirt, growling, wanting to join the fight, but stayed back.

I caught the alpha female stepping up to Jessup's side, and with the help of Gregory, who somehow made his way over, they helped him down from the pole. Were they readying him to escape if something happened?

Fenris bound forward, snapping his teeth at Nate's side. Nate shuffled quickly to the left, curling his head into Fenris and latching onto his ear, ripping it from his body. Fenris howled, leaving his neck unprotected. Nate clamped his massive jaw onto it and bit down. Fenris growled and whimpered, and when he rolled to the side, Nate held on, using his large paws to hold Fenris to the ground while he tore into Fenris's neck, ripping fur, skin, and muscles out.

As Fenris took his last breath, a howl started up around us.

The noise cut off when Nate moved off Fenris's dead body. He shifted back to his human body, crouching. When he straightened, naked, he used the back of his arm to wipe at his mouth. Not caring about his nudity, he turned around, gazing at each shifter.

"Anyone else want to challenge me?"

Not a sound was made.

I heard Alex click his fingers, and the blood on Nate disappeared. There were still scrapes and bruises, which would heal, but he looked better. Nate was also dressed in jeans once more. It seemed Alex was as jealous as I was, noticing the female shifters eyeing Nate. I liked I wasn't the only one worrying or being possessive of the men. I'd gladly have Alex's help, and I enjoyed, a lot, knowing there was something going on with the both of them. It made me hope all of my bonded mates would have the same type of connection with each other. I also had to admit, it turned me on and had me thinking I would very much like to see them together.

I caught Nate smirk at Alex before he looked toward Jessup, who stood with the assistance of the female alpha and Gregory.

"The pack is still yours," he said.

Jessup nodded. "The Falk pack appreciates the assistance. We'd also like to extend an offer to you to join our pack and become our beta."

My heart faltered.

Would he accept?

Did he miss being in a pack surrounded by his own kind?

Hands on my shoulders had me jolting. Alex's scent and heat touched me next as he molded his front to my back. Together, we stood there waiting for Nate's reply. Both anxious.

Nate glanced back to us, his eyes moved to Asher and even Thorn, then back to Alex and me. He faced Jessup again. "Thank you for the generous offer, but I already have my own pack."

My body relaxed into Alex, and I felt his muscles loosen as he slid his arms around my chest. He kissed the side of my head.

Jessup smiled. "I can see that."

"Why don't you all come in for a coffee?" the alpha female asked.

Coffee? Right now? What I wanted was to take my mates back to the castle, yell at Nate a little, and then have them surround me in bed, so I knew they were okay. I wanted them, all of them, to rest with me. I hadn't had them all in the same bed by myself. Usually it had been just Asher and Thorn together or by themselves. But I needed Alex and Nate to join us that night.

"It would be so they could talk privately about things," Alex said into my ear.

Nate glanced to me. I nodded.

"Lead the way," Nate told her. We slowly followed Jessup and her up to the biggest cabin.

"Please wait on the porch," I said to the guards.

They bowed, and one replied, "Yes, my queen."

When I walked in, with Alex at my side, the others were already seated around a living room, except for the alpha female. I could hear clattering in the kitchen. I pecked Alex on the cheek and made my way in there to help her.

"Can I help?" I asked in the doorway.

She glanced over her shoulder, her brows rising. "I didn't think the queen would lower herself to—"

"You don't know this queen. I still pick up my own laundry."

She turned back around, but I didn't miss her smile. "Amelie," she offered.

I walked over and helped with some mugs of coffee, since I knew how my guys took their drinks. "Hi, Amelie, I'm Paige."

"It would have been good to meet you properly under different circumstances."

"I agree, and I'm sorry for... your loss." After all, Fenris was her son.

She frowned. "I can't say it was a loss."

Well, okay then. "Should we get these into the room?"

"Yes. They'll be waiting on us."

She was right. As we entered, the room was quiet. I squeezed through the gap between the couches that were in an L-shape looking toward the wall where a large TV was fixed above a fireplace. I put the tray down on the coffee table and then handed out the drinks to my men before taking my own and sitting between Asher and Nate. Thorn and Alex stood behind the couch we were on while Jessup, Gregory, and Amelie were opposite us on their own couch.

The cabin felt warm and homey, especially with the knitted blankets flung over the back of each couch.

"Do you have someone else who can step up as beta?" Nate asked. His leg bounced up and down. He seemed on edge, but I had a feeling it had to do with the overflowing adrenaline from the fight.

"Yes, there are a few candidates." Jessup glanced at Amelie. When she nodded, he looked back to Nate. "The former queen allowed us onto her property because she trusted us to keep an eye on the outer regions. It gave our pack something to do, a purpose. There are many packs that would step into the role quickly if they knew about this community. We want to make sure the Falk pack is imbedded at the queen's side if the community grows."

Meaning, they wanted to stay in the position they were in and didn't want me to allow other packs to take their role if more were to flock to our area.

Why wasn't he asking me, though? Why wasn't he looking at me? Was it some wolf thing?

"You said our queen had to prove herself in the role before you followed her. Has she? Would you be faithful to her and her own?" Asher asked. "We won't risk our mate for anything."

Amelie stood. "With the changes she's already made and assisting us because one of her own asked for help, it has proven Paige Alice is more queen than the one before. She is humble, smart, fierce, and a woman who would fight for not only hers but others to make sure everyone is treated the same. We would follow, stand by, protect, and risk our own lives to make sure she is safe." She bowed. Jessup, with Gregory's help, stood and bowed as well.

"Thank you," I said, my voice soft. My cheeks heated. They saw me in a light I would never see myself in. I appreciated their kind words. "I would love to have the Falk pack at my side." Amelia and Jessup straightened, both smiling until I added, "However, I have a question."

They froze. "Yes?" Jessup said.

"Will Gregory be safe here? Will the pack care you're mated to a ghoul who's a man?"

Gregory's eyes filled with tears. "Thank you for caring, my queen."

"I will always care about my people." I smiled warmly.

Jessup took Gregory's hand. I looked to him as he said, "I'll make sure Gregory is safe here. Fenris was the leader of the few who hated same-sex matings and other races mixing."

"With him gone, we'll have things back in order," Amelie said.

Jessup nodded. "We will."

"My queen," Gregory called. "I would still like to work in the castle, if you'll allow it?"

"Of course, Gregory. I'd be lost without you." I smiled. While his grin was back, it was wobbly and soft.

Nate suddenly stood. "Now that's settled, we're going," he stated roughly.

Jessup and Amelie shared a look, one full of knowing. Jessup chuckled. "Of course, I'm surprised you handled it this long."

"Handled what?" I asked, also standing.

"Nothing," Nate clipped.

"Nate." I glared. "I thought you'd be in a better mood since winning out there, but it doesn't seem like it." It was then I punched him in the stomach.

"What the fuck?" he yelled.

"That's for scaring me, you asshole."

"Are they always like this?" I heard Jessup ask.

"Yes," Alex, Thorn, and Asher replied together.

"I had it handled," Nate seethed through clenched teeth in my face.

"I know that now," I yelled, "but I freaked out at the time. Do you know how hard it was to stand back and watch?"

"Yes," he hissed. "It's about as hard as it is watching you risk your life."

I jerked my head back. All right, he had a point. "Hmm, well, okay. But tell me what you need to handle now."

Nate scrubbed a hand over his face while others laughed around us. Nate sighed. His hands landed on my arms, and I was pushed back into Asher. He then walked around the couch, got near Alex, bent and flung Alex over his shoulder and slapped his ass. Alex cried out in surprise.

"Bring her," Nate clipped.

"What's going on?" I demanded.

"Wolves like to fuck after a fight," Amelie stated with humor in her voice.

My mouth dropped open. Nate glowered over at me. "You wanted to watch, right?"

I was sure the biggest smile I'd ever had covered my mouth. I jumped at Asher. Thankfully he caught me in bridal style. "Let's go!"

CHAPTER SIX
NATE

Alex didn't complain as I raced through the woods back to the castle with him over my shoulder. Asher, with Paige in his arms, who giggled like a maniac, and Thorn, kept to my pace. Alex gripped my waist and held on. He didn't say anything until we got close to the opened area.

"You need to put me down."

"What the fuck for?" I demanded. I didn't want him away from me; he was the only one I'd claimed, the only one I knew who was willing to let me fuck them the way I wanted —rough and hard—so I wasn't letting him from my reach.

He smacked my ass. "People will see. It's bad enough the guards and wolves did. We can't have the people know… know about, ah… you know." I just knew he'd be blushing beet red.

Was he worried about himself or me?

"If you don't—"

"No, I don't care, but we should put up a pretense—"

"Alex," Paige called. With his hands digging into my butt, Alex lifted himself enough to capture her gaze. "Fuck them," she announced, and shit, I wanted to laugh.

"But—"

She shook her head. "I'm queen. I rule here, not them, and until that changes, I, as well as all of you, can do what we like when it comes to our relationships. Don't hide your feelings for anyone. Please. If they don't like it, they can leave."

"Okay," Alex replied in a whisper. It was fucking sweet he'd been worried, but I didn't give a shit what anyone thought, and neither did my wolf. If we wanted to take our mates in the middle of a field, we would.

We ran out into the clearing. It was late, and only a few people were scattered around the area. They watched us until we disappeared through the castle gates. Some frowned, a lot smiled, and there was even a chuckle or two when they realized, from Paige waving, that there wasn't anything wrong.

Before we knew it, I had the door to Paige's room open and was stepping through, allowing Alex to drop to his feet. He started to step back until I hauled him back close to me with a growl in the back of my throat.

His eyes widened as he looked up at me. I heard the door close, but I didn't move my gaze from Alex, who licked his lips. As I watched his tongue, another rumble fell from between my lips.

Paige wanted to watch—something I fucking loved the thought of. Especially since the room was already mixed with her sweet scent of arousal from just seeing Alex and me close.

Leaning in, I pressed my mouth against Alex's. I heard Paige gasp, and as I opened Alex's mouth by nipping at his bottom lip, another hit of arousal scented the room. Alex's hands tightened on my hips. Our heads tilted this way and that. I couldn't get enough of kissing him. It still surprised the fuck out of me. Kissing a guy, a team member, but hell, he was my mate. He knew what he was getting into with me, and he'd accepted it.

I slid my hand from the back of his neck down to cup his ass cheek and squeezed. He let out a whimper and tore his mouth from mine, panting. His hooded gaze lifted to mine and then moved over to the others in the room. I looked there too.

My heart gave a lurch.

Thorn stood behind Paige. His hand was down in her pants and her legs shook. She gripped his arm as if it were the only thing that held her up. Asher, without a shirt, sat on the bed. His hand ran up and down his length behind his slacks.

Alex stopped breathing for a moment seeing it, until I grabbed him and turned him like Thorn had Paige. His heart thudded hard in his chest when I slowly glided my hand into his jeans. He moaned when I threaded my hand round his erection and leisurely dragged it up and down him.

"Take her to the bed," I ordered.

Thorn smirked. He withdrew his hand, and I knew Alex, like me, was watching. When Thorn licked his fingers clean, Alex's cock throbbed in my hand while mine jerked in my jeans. Asher stood, his slacks dropped to the floor, and he stepped out of them, kicking them away.

Naked.

Asher was fucking naked in front of us. He stepped out of the way so Thorn could help Paige onto the bed. She lay at the head of the bed, watching us all with lust burning in her eyes. She bit her bottom lip when Asher kneeled on the bed, helping her get rid of her top, and Thorn removed her pants, gliding them down her legs at an unrushed pace.

Jesus Christ.

Thorn moved back to get rid of his own clothes, and Alex and I got a full view of Paige bare on the bed.

Claim her. Fuck her. Mark her. My wolf rumbled over and over in my head.

Alex sucked in a sharp breath, and I realized I held him a little tight. I released my grip, removed my hand and then helped him take off his shirt. His arms lifted automatically, and I threw the fabric to the floor. Paige, up on her elbows, watched me as I slid my hands over Alex's smooth skin, savoring his hard muscles.

I popped the button to his jeans, and—Alex clicked his fingers. His and my jeans disappeared. Our cocks shot up. I chuckled, as did Asher and Thorn at Alex's eagerness. Over his shoulder, I caught his face heating. I bit my mark on his skin and thrust my hips into his ass cheeks. "Don't get embarrassed in here," I told him.

"I agree," Paige said. I glanced over. A growl dropped from my lips when I saw she had her fingers playing with her clit. "It's hot, how excited you get," she said, her voice low and thick with desire.

Alex nodded. He took my hand and pulled it down to his dick. Smiling, I grabbed his erection and jerked him up and down. I curled my other arm around his chest and nipped at his shoulder before licking there. My mark was still on him. It would stay there forever, and I fucking loved seeing it.

With my body, I gently pushed him over to the bed, still jacking him with each step we took.

"Please," Paige whispered. She was drenched below, and seeing it, scenting it, the wolf and I wanted to lick her juices clean.

"P-Please what?" Alex asked.

Only she didn't answer because Asher slid onto the bed, pressing beside her and taking her nipple into his mouth. Thorn sat at the end of the mattress and ran his hand up and down her calves. Her legs spread under his touch. Her scent was intoxicating.

Overwhelmed, I pushed Alex's upper body forward. Before his hands landed on the bed, he clicked his fingers, and a tube of lube landed on the bed near us. Thorn picked it up and went to pass it, but he got too close to Alex, and my wolf and I didn't like it. A low snarl sounded out of me. He paused, his eyes widening.

Alex pushed his ass back onto me, grabbed the lube and lifted it over his shoulder. I snatched it out of his hand and opened it, rubbing it over my length and then Alex's hole. Immediately, he backed into my touch.

"It's all right. He didn't touch me," Alex said softly, probably because I couldn't stop the rattle of my growl in my chest. Alex cleared his throat.

"Why…?" Paige trailed off when I turned Alex enough for her to see I had my fingers inside Alex, stretching him. Alex's head dropped. I could hear his ragged breathing easily and the little mew sound Paige made.

Asher kissed her shoulder. "Because his wolf is as possessive as the man is, and he doesn't like his mate being touched by others."

Paige's head tilted. She may not have realized it, but she leaned closer our way, her gaze riveted on where I toyed with Alex. "But… he didn't mind me touching him."

Asher cupped her breast, tweaking her nipple with his fingers, and her breath hitched. "That's because he knows you'll be his sooner or later. Thorn and I are more dominant —" I snorted, then gnashed my teeth at him. Asher smirked. "He doesn't trust us completely to not take away what's his. That is, until he's claimed us."

Shock radiated over my wolf and I. It had me removing my fingers. Alex let out a complaint and glared over at Asher.

Thorn smiled, and I caught Asher's brow rising. "That is what will happen, right? Your wolf sees us all as his?" I nodded once, waiting for his reaction. Asher's eyes bled to green, his fangs dropping. "We'll have to see who gets topped, wolf. I don't give in easily."

My upper lip rose, and my claws flashed out. The half change came over me. My body grew, my hair lengthened, and my teeth sharpened. The wolf and I were one in body. "I'll take you on and make you mine, vampire."

Asher snarled. "We will see."

Alex groaned, but in annoyance. "Can we have a pissing contest later? We've got better things to—" He cried out when we entered him, our pink tip sliding further into him, in our half form. He was right. We had better things to do. We'd take Asher and force him to heel later. We'd do the same to Thorn if he wanted to fight for dominance as well.

Paige's heart took off in flight. She rubbed her legs together but then spread them when Thorn was back to rubbing his hand up her leg. She licked her lips and then bit the bottom one as we pulled back out of a panting Alex, then thrust back in again. We gripped his hips hard and pounded into our first mate, who accepted us with ease, even when he was damn tight.

Thorn sat with one leg on the bed, the other hanging off the bed with his foot planted on the floor. Paige let out a squeal when Thorn pulled her down the bed a little by her calves. He dipped down and licked her wetness, eating her like she was his favorite ice cream. She squirmed under him. Her mouth dropped open in a silent moan. Alex pushed back on me hard—he liked watching Thorn devour Paige's pussy.

She reached out under Alex, and when he uttered, "Fucking hell." We knew she was jerking him off. Blindly, she sought out Asher with her other hand and wrapped it around his large length, tracing her grip up and down.

It was lucky we knew she was going to be ours. We knew she wouldn't fight when it came time to claim. So we let her have attention from her other mates. Alex leaned in and took her left nipple into his mouth, while Asher took her right. She gasped and bared down on Thorn's mouth. All while we fucked Alex from behind.

The sight… Christ, it was amazing. We wanted to howl in pleasure.

Thorn pulled back and shoved at Asher, moving him enough so Thorn could pick Paige up. He shifted her around our way. Alex swore again when he looked down at her pussy.

"Get him on the bed," Thorn ordered.

We embedded our dick in Alex, causing him to groan, and with our hand on his hips, we ushered him forward, so he moved closer to the bed. We pushed him lower as Paige wiggled down the bed more.

"Will you let me finish the bond, Alex?" Paige asked huskily.

"Yes," he hissed.

We threaded our hand between Paige and Alex. Gripping his dick, we held it against her entrance. Pulling our cock out of him, we pushed in and forced him to slide right inside of Paige. Both screamed at the same time. When Alex stilled, we panicked and went to grab him.

Thorn snatched our arms and shook his head. "Let the bond connect."

We ground our teeth together. We didn't like to see either of them so still. Alex grunted. At the sound, we shook off Thorn's hold and went for Alex again—something smashed into us, and we were ripped away from Alex, landing on the floor with a thud. We heard Asher say, "Relax, it's okay. They're okay. They'll fight it out. Just keep going."

Sounds of flesh slapping against flesh filled the room. Alex groaned and Paige gasped. We knew they were good, they were together, fulfilling the bond. We wanted to see but were beyond pissed at being held back. With a roar, we rolled the weight off us, our hands wrapping around Thorn's neck as we squeezed. His grin was fucking evil right before his fist landed on our cheek. Our head snapped to the side. We let out a low, deep growl.

"Yes. God, yes, Alex," Paige cried. We paused, raised our head, and looked over to see Alex drilling into Paige, and yet she still yelled, "Harder."

He did, and then next, Paige screamed his name. We scented her cum just before Alex cursed, then grunted, "I'm coming."

Thorn pushed us to the side. He went to stand, but we grabbed him around the waist and pulled him under us. Alex moved onto the bed; he was okay. He picked Paige up and seated her between his legs. He kissed her neck, and she smiled lazily. Wrapping his arms around Paige's waist, they both looked down at us on the floor.

We'd been distracted enough to have Thorn buck us off him. He had time to grab the edge of the bed before we hauled his body back toward me. We flipped him over, and his fist connected with our fucking face again. We wrapped our hand around his wrist and slapped it to the floor. We snatched his other arm and brought both up above his head.

Leaning down, we snarled in his face. It pissed us off even more when he laughed. We spotted the lube on the floor near us. We'd give the fucker something to laugh about.

Yes. Fuck, claim. Make him ours.

Thorn's eyes widened when we took both his wrists in one hand and then clasped the bottle. He tried to shove us off, but we quickly flicked the lid open and used our knees to spread his legs, squirting the substance on him. Thorn's eyes glowed red, and he struggled against our hold. We heard a bone snap in his wrist, yet we didn't let go.

"It's fine, Paige. They both like it," Asher whispered.

Thorn lifted his head, snapping his sharp teeth at us. We gnashed ours back before we rested our chest against his. Using our knees, spreading his apart more, we pushed a hand under his ass, lifting enough to slam our cock inside him.

"Ours," we clipped roughly as he stilled. We pulled out and thrust in. Our mate clenched around us and let out a deep, grunting moan.

We smiled wickedly. He liked it. He wanted it, and we'd give it to him.

We withdrew again and rolled forward inside his heat. Thorn's eyes closed, his mouth parting. We could see his sharp teeth. Then a noise caught our attention. We looked up and spotted the vampire behind our soon-to-be female mate fucking her while she watched us and sucked on our mate's cock.

Our chest vibrated with a noise. Conflicted, we wanted to continue watching them, but the beast under us got a hand free and raked his claws down our chest. Roaring, we grabbed his arm and pulled it away to bend and latch our mouth onto his shoulder.

"Ours," I told him around his skin.

"Yes," he moaned.

With our teeth sinking into his flesh, Thorn cried out as we fucked him faster. We kept our teeth in him so the mark would stay, so people would see he was ours. His legs rose over our hips, holding on while we pounded into him.

We shifted our eyes in time to see our mate holding Paige's head and crying out through his release into her mouth. The vampire kept an eye on us even as he took his pleasure, even as he gripped the female tighter to him. She licked our mate one last time and then reached back to grip the vampire's neck, holding on as he drilled his dick into her wet pussy.

"Asher," she yelled as her orgasm scented the room again just before the vampire bared his teeth and pulled out of her to spread his ejaculating seed onto the female's skin.

"Nate," our mate under us whispered. "Faster."

We growled around his skin. Wanting to please our mate, we fucked him with everything we had. His hands landed on our ass, holding us, gripping us.

"Fuck, coming," he bit out.

He tightened around us more, drawing out our end, and we came inside him. Spent, relaxed, and damn happy, the wolf receded, my body shrank, and I slipped from Thorn. He let out a noise but rubbed his hands up and down my back. I released my teeth from his skin and licked at the bite. Pulling back, I peered down at it, and I felt a bark of pleasure from my wolf at the sight of our mark still there after his skin healed.

I moved my gaze down to capture Thorn's; he was back to his normal self. He didn't seem fazed by me claiming him; he just stared back, his eyes light with humor. Then he lifted his head and pressed his lips against mine. Shock hit me, but then I deepened the kiss, sliding my hand to the back of his head.

"I can't wait to see the wolf take on the vampire," Paige commented from the bed.

Breaking the kiss, I pecked at Thorn's lips once more before looking up. First, I checked on Alex, to make sure he was okay and fine with the new connection the wolf and I had made. Alex smiled down at me as he ran his fingers through Paige's hair.

Then I looked to Asher, who seemed amused, if the smirk was anything to go by. "Yes," he said. "It shall be entertaining. Hard to tell who will win, though."

I let out a huff, ignoring his taunt because the wolf and I were confident we'd best him. I stood, holding out my hand to Thorn. He took it, and I pulled him to his feet. I ran a hand over the side of his face. Content to have him as a mate, yet I still wanted more that night.

I was tired of fighting it.

My wolf agreed with me on my next thought.

Yes, he roared.

This was our destiny. This was our pack.

The vampire I would get to eventually, but for now, it was time to complete the bond.

I needed Paige.

I had to claim her.

Her whole being spoke to me in ways I'd never had. She drove me fucking insane, but I couldn't see my life now without her. Without any of them. I glanced at Paige. "I'm going for a shower. Are you too tired to finalize the bond with me?"

She gulped. Heat hit her cheeks, and before worry could steal my breath, she shook her head and said, "I'm not tired. I would like that."

"Good," I grunted.

With that organized, I walked toward the joined bathroom with a smile on my face and my dick already growing at the thought of being inside her.

CHAPTER SEVEN
PAIGE

"Should I shower as well?" I asked nervously after Nate disappeared into the en suite. The door opened again, and Nate stuck his head out.

His voice was rough and deep when he said, "No. Just clean your skin and the bed." The door slammed closed, and I glanced up at Alex.

His cheeks burned as he stammered, "Uh… he's, um, I mean… he's, as in, Nate is okay with my…" His brows rose. "…cum inside you, but he wants Asher's essence off you and the bed," he finished in a rush.

It was my turn to blush. Then I scolded myself for it because I shouldn't be embarrassed by what we'd done. Asher, and now Alex, were my mates, so we could do what we wanted with each other.

Asher laughed. "It seems, until the wolf can claim me—if he can and not the other way around—then we need to make sure I'm not scented around you while he claims you."

Oh.

I glanced to Thorn's neck to see the teeth marks there.

Thorn smiled. "It's okay, sweetheart. It didn't hurt." He actually stood straighter and seemed proud to have the mark. I still couldn't believe what I'd seen or how turned on I'd been watching Nate take Alex and then dominate Thorn. The way their bodies moved, the way they touched each other, fucked each other... dear God, if it was a TV show, I wouldn't get anything done. Instead, I would watch it every day and all day long. Just thinking of the way Nate's hips pistoned in and out of Alex and Thorn had me rubbing my thighs together. To top it all, bonding with Alex was more than I'd imagined. The way he held me down, the way he pinched my nipples and clit, the way he fucked me like I wanted was mind-blowing. I could feel him in me, feel the desire swirling inside him, the desire that had his dick growing right before my eyes.

I glanced up at him as he said, "It's you who has me hardening. I can sense how turned on you are. What were you thinking?"

I smiled sheepishly. "About us together and about Nate with you and Thorn."

Alex ran his thumb over my bottom lip. "You really don't mind Nate's claim? About us... fucking?" I'd never heard him swear; it was cute and yet sexy at the same time.

"I don't mind at all. I love getting pleasure but also seeing you all have it as well. If it's the five of us together or you with Nate alone and I hear about it, then I'm happy."

In the next second, I was on my back with Alex over me. "You really are amazing and meant to be ours, Paige Alice. I'm honored to be known as your bonded mate."

I cupped his cheeks, then ran my hands up through his hair before meeting his gaze again. "I'm glad, because I love you all the same."

His eyes closed. He sucked in a deep breath, and I felt his love pour into me. I gasped, arched up into him, and wrapped my arms around his neck, dragging him down to me to kiss him senseless. He rocked his erection into my hip. A throat cleared, but I was too lost in the sensation, in the scent of

Alex and his hard, smooth, wonderful skin while I glided my hands down his back.

"We should clean before the wolf—"

A hard, urgent knock sounded on the door. Alex and I froze. In the next blink, Alex clicked his fingers, and all of us were dressed and the bed was made with clean sheets.

"Enter," Asher barked.

The door swung open. A pale Felnick entered. "There's a problem, my queen."

I groaned, rubbing a hand over my face. "Another one? Is it Lucifer on the phone?"

"No. Our brothers-in-arms, who were sent out into the world, have found Selma. She's locked herself in a room with a few humans, threatening to kill them, and won't come out until she speaks with the queen in person."

"She's here?" Thorn questioned.

Felnick shook his head. "She's in New York."

The door to the en suite flew open, and Nate, only in a towel, stomped in. He pointed at me and snapped, "Don't even fucking think about going."

Bristling, my anger surfaced. I stood quickly with my hands on my hips, only realizing I was dressed in a snowsuit. It had me blinking down at it and then glancing over at Alex. His jaw unclenched enough to bite out, "No one has the right to see your skin after…." After I'd been thoroughly fucked, he left off, and I appreciated that he had. My face heated, while I heard Thorn and Asher chuckle, as Nate snorted.

It was sweet he was being protective.

"But a snowsuit?" I pressed.

"Yes." He nodded, and I had a feeling he wouldn't change my outfit even if I wanted him to.

Sighing, something I hadn't done in a while, I faced Nate

again. "If you weren't so hot and muscular, and tall, and good-looking with your warm skin—"

Someone cleared their throat loudly.

Damn Nate for distracting me with his body. My eyes narrowed even more at his smug smile. "If you weren't meant to be my bonded mate, I would so kick your ass right now for ordering me."

He rolled his eyes. "I'm here to protect you. I'll easily tie you to the bed if I have to."

That had me picturing it. Tied to the bed while he got all growly and bossy and assholey…. Wait, that couldn't mean I liked his hard-edge moods, right?

Fuck. I thought it did.

Still, I wouldn't let him get away with it.

"Ah, my queen," Felnick called.

"Yes?" I asked, facing him.

"What should we do about the issue?"

Right. Selma. Honestly, it wasn't a decision I could make on the fly. There was so much to consider. I glanced at my men, then asked, "What do you all think?"

"It's a trap," Nate declared.

"Something is amiss with the request," Asher said.

"Why would she leave the sanctuary to then ask to see you or she'll kill humans? She could have just spoken with you here," Alex pointed out.

"Like Nate said, it has to be a trap," Thorn added.

Thinning my lips, I nodded. Staring at the floor, I said quietly, "But I can't risk lives just because I'm worried it's a trap."

"Yes, you can," Nate boomed. "You're queen. Your life is worth more than anyone's. You're the change for the future. The people need you above anyone here."

I shook my head. "I'm not above anyone's life. Everyone is important."

"My queen, if I may?" Felnick asked, his head bowed.

"Yes?"

"It is honorable you would even think to risk yourself for others. The way you already protect your people, allowing them to live their lives fully and by taking the harshness that darkens some doorsteps is beyond what some queens would do. You do not see your life more important than any others, so it's our job to do it for you. Already, I can foretell that if something happened to you, everything would fall into the pits of Hell. People like Odin, Barrett, or the members of the council would take over, would rule cruelly. If you would allow us to care for your life, like you would others, to protect the good you will do in this world, then it is a task we'll take on happily."

If I didn't think my men would harm Felnick, I would have thrown my arms around him and hugged him tightly. The way he saw me shocked me, but how could I risk my life after that speech?

"She's leaking," Nate clipped. "You fucking made her leak." He stomped toward Felnick. Thorn wrapped his arms around Nate's chest and held him tightly, while Felnick backed into the wall. It had me wondering again about how Felnick could be fierce and protective against anyone but Lucifer, during the phone call, and my bonded. Then again, my men were badasses, and I was sure Lucifer could make anyone piss themselves, and I didn't even know the man, devil, whatever.

Arms circled my waist. Alex stood at my back before he leaned in to kiss my neck. Asher stepped close and took my hand in his, running his thumb over my skin; both had me sniffing and closing my eyes to compose myself before Nate killed Felnick.

"Look, she's fine. Her bonded calmed her," Thorn told Nate.

I opened my eyes as Nate glanced our way. He took me in from head to toe first before he glanced to Alex and Asher. Then his upper lip raised at my vampire until Asher stepped back a little, away from Alex. Rolling my eyes, I stated, "And you said I was crazy when it came to claiming and being possessive."

He growled low. My clit twinged as if that growl had been just for her.

If only we hadn't been interrupted with this new situation, because by now, I would have finished the bond with my annoying and arrogant wolf. Still, it was something to look forward to.

Sorrow stabbed at my chest.

Ezra.

I'd forgotten all about his loss, so guilt twisted my heart painfully.

"Paige," Alex whispered. "It's okay—"

"Leave us for a moment, Felnick," Thorn ordered. "We'll have an answer on what to do soon."

He bowed and backed out of the room, closing the door behind him.

"I should feel guilty for forgetting him, right?" My eyes misted again when I looked up at Asher.

"Fucking hell. She's leaking again." I ignored Nate's mutter and the need to slap him because Alex wrapped me up tighter, right before there was a bright light and a feeling of weightlessness. Next, I was sitting on the bed between Alex's spread legs. He gently pulled my back against his chest. With a click of his fingers, I was redressed in shorts and a T-shirt.

My other men approached. Thorn sat on my left, Asher on the right, while Nate stood at the end of the bed with his arms crossed over his chest, glaring down at us. Yet I could still see the concern in his eyes. He hated when I was upset, and knowing he felt something showed me more about the mate he would be. Already I knew he was protective to a point he would tie me up. He could be sweet, happy, and amazing like he'd been whenever he was around Alex.

Thorn reached his hand out to Nate, whose jaw clenched when he gazed down at it, then stopped. I caught a faint smile before Nate took Thorn's hand. They shared a look, one that was full of heat and tenderness. One I wanted to witness all the time between every single one of my bonded.

"Paige?" Alex whispered as his hand sifted through my hair.

"I'm sorry. For a moment I forgot about Ezra. The sorrow slammed into me, and then the guilt over forgetting took over."

"You don't have to feel guilty, love," Asher said, taking my hand in both of his. "You're not forgetting him. You never will. There'll be times in your day when you're distracted, where you'll smile, laugh, and even feel the best pleasure of your life." His brows rose, and I couldn't help but laugh even when tears dropped onto my cheeks. "But the loss of Ezra will always be inside you, and when you feel other things, it only means you've pushed it back enough to live in the moment. It means you're living, love."

My bottom lip trembled, yet I nodded. "I know you're right…. It's just… when I remember, it hurts."

"And it will for a very long time," Thorn said.

"But we'll be at your side to help you through that pain," Alex mumbled against my temple.

Nate grunted. When I looked up at him, he nodded.

"Fate really did the best job in her life when she put us all together," I told them, smiling softly.

"I agree," Alex said. The rest grinned over at me, though Nate's was more of a smug smirk.

"Now, what are we going to do about the Selma situation?" Alex asked.

"I have a feeling if I say I want to go see what she has to say, you'll all lock me in a tower."

"Damn right," Nate growled.

Shaking my head at him, I glanced at Thorn. "Do you think your brotherhood could get in there without the humans being harmed?"

"Vampires are faster, sweetheart. I'm afraid there will be some casualties."

That was what I feared as well.

"I could go," Alex announced, and coldness washed through me.

"No," I cried. Turning, I placed my hands on his cheeks and said again, "No. If none of you will let me risk myself, then I won't let any of you do the same."

His hands landed over mine, and he smiled. "I have skills that some may not even know of. I'm strong, Paige. I was top of my class. Why do you think Asher selected me right out of school? I can do this easily."

"I'll go with him," Thorn said, and I swung my gaze to his. Tears already pooled in my eyes. I blinked them away and let them fall onto my skin.

"I've already lost Ezra. I can't lose either of you."

Alex's hand traced up and down my back while I kept them both in sight. "You won't. Have faith in us."

"Why can't the brotherhood just go in?"

"There's a high chance there'll be fewer casualties with Alex there," Nate stated. "He's good at what he does." Alex preened at Nate's words, his chest puffing out, and a wide grin overtook his mouth.

Fear still held me back from agreeing. It felt like my throat had closed off, suffocating the words they wanted to hear because I didn't want them to go.

But then… I had to believe in them, in their skills. Before we'd even met, they were soldiers. They did this type of thing every day. Even though I wanted to lock them up in their own tower, I knew I couldn't suffocate their abilities.

I had to trust them to come back to me.

Clearing my throat, I opened my mouth, choked, and then cleared my throat again. Finally, I nodded. "Okay," I whispered. "I trust you both to come back to me in one piece, or else I'll find a way to bring you back and make your lives a living hell."

Tears erupted in my eyes once more, panic seizing my body. Then Alex dragged me back into his arms, hugging me close. He kissed my head. It wasn't enough, so I tilted my head and captured his lips with my own.

"Promise me you'll stay safe," I said against them.

"I promise." He nodded.

Looking to Thorn, I reached my hand out to him. He crawled onto the bed and moved my way before hovering over me as I lay back onto Alex's chest. "Promise me you'll keep safe."

"I vow to you I will do everything in my power to come back."

With my hand to the back of his neck, I drew him down and kissed him just as fiercely as I had Alex. My heart raced behind my ribs. I hated the thought of them leaving the community, the safe sanctuary we had here.

My hands trembled as I loosened my grip on Thorn. He moved back and stood beside the bed, smiling warmly down at me. Alex lifted me, and I was in Asher's arms. They wound around me as Asher sat me on his lap, and then Alex got off the bed to stand beside Thorn.

"I'll walk them out," Nate said, his voice hard and rough. He disliked this as much as I did.

However, I nodded. "I want to be updated every half hour until you're both back here with us."

"We will," Alex said. "No trap will keep us from coming home."

"You'd better be right," I told him.

They made their way to the door, opened it, and walked out. Nate gave us a look before he closed it after them.

"Did I do the right thing by letting them go?"

"Yes," Asher whispered.

"Then why does it feel like I didn't?" My face stung with the number of tears that bombarded my eyes. I bit my bottom lip to stop the tremble.

"Because you love them, and it will never be easy to watch them walk into battle, but you're strong enough to know you're doing the right thing to save all the lives you can." His hand threaded into my hair, and he tipped my head back with a gentle tug. "It doesn't mean you have to stay strong behind closed doors when I'm here to catch you."

With that, I buried my face into his chest and cried.

CHAPTER EIGHT
ALEX

With the bond between Paige and I complete, I finally felt like my feet were firmly set on the ground. I hadn't realized I'd been floating around the world missing something until the moment Nate claimed me and one foot got placed down. But then, when Paige's power bonded us together, my other foot solidly got pushed to the ground.

My life, my purpose, finally made sense. I was theirs and they were mine. I also felt like I belonged to Thorn and Asher. Even with my own family, I hadn't sensed being wanted, needed, or loved... until now. Until my new family.

All because of Paige.

I couldn't thank Fate enough for choosing me to be a part of something so important, giving me people I would cherish for the rest of my long existence.

Smiling, I glanced to Nate and Thorn as we stood in the war room with Felnick and twenty other brothers-in-arms. Thorn had just informed them that he and I would be involved in the capture of Selma. Nate had stated how Paige wouldn't be joining us before anyone else could question it; there wasn't a chance we'd let Paige out into the world. There was too much at risk. We still didn't know why the demons had been after her in the first place or who sent them. Or were they working on their own accord?

Before we entered the war room, I'd voiced my other concerns—ones Nate and Asher would have to keep an eye on. Grace, the coven mistress who had been against Paige's changes for the community, hadn't as yet done anything to move against Paige, and even though we'd made sure to keep up to date with Agatha, a witch who was keeping tabs on her coven mistress for us, there was still a risk something could happen to Paige because of that woman.

Nate, in his grumpy way, told me he wasn't that stupid. Of course he'd keep an eye on things.

"Thorn and I will transport to the hotel she's holed up in and scout the area before entering."

"Is it advisable for the queen's bonded males to go into battle?" one of the guards from the brotherhood said.

Thorn snapped his gaze the guard's way. "Just because we're mated to the queen doesn't mean we'd sit on our asses and let everything go to shit when we have the strength and the power to help."

The guard bowed. "Of course, sire."

"Now I understand why Paige is against being bowed at and called queen. I'll never get used to being called sire," Thorn grumbled. He moved to the wall of weapons and strapped on some knives and guns. My magic was my weapon. Hands touched my thigh. Startled, I swung my gaze down to see Nate fitting me with a thigh holster.

My pulse raced. I wanted to smile, to gush even, but that would piss him off. "What are you doing?"

"Shut up. Just fucking humor me like you did when Asher ordered you to carry one weapon. Know you're strong in magic, Alex, but for my own sanity,"—he shoved a gun into the holster—"you're taking this."

I ran my hand over his shoulder. "All right." I couldn't help but grin since he'd never worried like this about me before, but now we were mated, he was a wreck. I didn't wipe the grin away quick enough. When Nate looked up at me, he growled low and kept doing so when he slowly stood in front of me.

The room quieted, sensing the rising pissed-off wolf.

His hand gripped the back of my neck, and he slammed his mouth onto me in a hard, punishing but delicious kiss. He broke it when he sensed Thorn close because in a blink, Thorn crashed into us, and Nate was kissing him too.

When Nate broke the kiss, his eyes were dark, his wolf there, and he ordered in a dark voice, "Have each other's back. Come home. Pack first."

"Pack first," I told him.

"We'll come back," Thorn reassured him. He stared at us both before snarling, turning, and walking out of the room.

"He… the wolf… I've never—"

"Never what?" Thorn snapped.

The guard blanched. "Never seen a wolf take more than one mate," he blurted.

"Congratulations, sire," Felnick offered.

Thorn smiled. "Thank you, brother." I didn't know much about Thorn, and I needed that to change. What I did know was that he was a respected, good man. One Nate's wolf claimed without question. And that told me a lot more than anything else. Nate didn't take people into his pack easily. But it seemed knowing Thorn was Paige's also made the choice simple. We were now in each other's lives forever.

It was definitely time to get to know him.

* * *

With a hold on Thorn, I transported us into a corner of the lobby in the hotel Selma had selected to stay. There were already members of Thorn's brotherhood in the surveillance room and dotted throughout the hotel waiting for us. I drew in the power that escaped on the transport and then blocked Thorn and our essence. We didn't want to give away we'd arrived to anyone who was working with Selma.

"You said you didn't know much about the vampire, but do you think she would sink low enough to work with demons to trap Paige?" I asked as we walked toward the surveillance room, only to come to an abrupt halt. Snapping my hand out, I took hold of Thorn's arm.

He spun back to me. "What?"

"Magic and—" Doors crashed open. "—demons," I called over the noise of all different types and sizes of demons rushing into the room snarling, growling. "Ready?"

"Always," Thorn yelled. His eyes changed to red, while mine shifted to purple as I called my powers forward. Thorn grabbed the guns from his hips and fired at the fast-approaching demons. A lot fell to the floor, but not enough. I swept my hand out, picking up at least ten of them, flinging them into the wall. Bones breaking echoed around the room. My lips moved over a spell, and knives shot out of my palms, aiming at the closest demons.

Thorn's gun fired over and over until he ran out and threw them to the floor, grabbing two others. I shot off another spell, telling him, "They shouldn't run out of bullets."

His grin over his shoulder was wild and wicked since his teeth had sharpened from his ghoul side. "Thanks." He went back to shooting everything he spotted while I blinded the monsters with a sunshine spell. They screeched and screamed, covering their eyes, giving Thorn more time to shoot a lot of them. When that spell faded, I had another ready. The floor liquefied, and demons sank into it, crying out in surprise. They clawed at the ground once it solidified.

I moved my eyes to the door when another wave of demons crawled, ran, and flew in. They were stronger ones. When a ball of fire flew my way, I swiped it to the side and shot off my own. It hit him, only he smiled as the flames ran over his body.

Fuck.

Since fire didn't work, I formed a spell for ice and engaged it. The demon's eyes widened. He dodged right, but I already had another two erupting from my palms. One hit him. He howled in pain and sank to his knees, frosting over.

A hit to my back had me stumbling forward. My back burned. I crafted a spell to heal whatever had me in agony. Pain still laced through me as I turned to see Grace standing there smiling.

"Now," she yelled, and two other witches stepped up to her sides.

Anger had my feet lifting off the floor, had me spreading my hands, had wild wind whipping around me. My lips moved, but no sound came from them as I locked onto their own spell and broke it apart inch by inch. I managed to glance at Thorn, checking he was okay. His eyes were wide watching me. He wasn't focused and demons approached.

"Behind you," I said, my voice hard.

He spun in time to decapitate the two heads off the demon, then sliced another down the middle. He must have lost his guns at some point to be using the swords he'd had strapped to his back.

The witches staggered a step forward, bringing a smile to my face. "You won't best me," I told them.

Grace's brow dipped in concentration. She changed up her spell, and I quickly countered it with my own alteration, using my hands in the air, drawing patterns and swirls.

Grace let out an agitated scream.

"Where is Selma?" I demanded.

Grace swiped at her forehead and laughed. "Not here." She smiled. "She was never here," she said, her voice different.

"That's Selma's voice," Thorn called. He leaped to the other side of me and attacked the demons there, his blade effortlessly cutting through an acid ball shot his way.

"Do you know where Selma is?" I asked.

"She had other orders," a new voice said. A man stepped out of a darkened corner. He licked his lips, his eyes glowing red. "You have delicious power." He looked at Grace. "I want them both."

"The mage is strong—"

"You promised to make it happen," the demon roared.

Grace frowned and nodded.

The demon smiled and gazed up at me. "I'll be seeing and playing with you both soon." His eyes shifted to the others in the room. "Those who drag them down into Hell will be rewarded." Then he vanished.

Grace cried out. A fog floated up around her, and she laughed maniacally.

Jesus, she was gaining more power.

"You don't have to do this," I told Grace.

"I feel amazing." She smiled, then pulled the witch to her left close and sliced her throat open. Grace's lips moved. She grabbed the other screaming witch and stabbed her in the heart.

Blood magic was the darkest. Fear pierced my chest. I could maybe counter it, but I didn't have the time, and I had to keep our promise to Paige and Nate.

"Thorn, to me," I yelled, landing back on the floor. Thorn wrapped his arms around me. I went to transport us out, but nothing happened. The floor beneath us vanished as Grace opened a portal straight to Hell. I gripped Thorn to me and floated above it. Demons surrounded us. I pushed them back magically, but more ran in. There was a pop—my protective bubble fell away. Three demons jumped at us before I could get us high enough. They locked their arms around our legs, and then there was a clap and we were being dragged into the portal.

Into Hell.

Blackness surrounded us as we kept falling. Thorn released his hold and pushed off me to wrap himself around a demon and sliced over and over with his claws at his chest. The demon screamed in pain and fury before exploding. He went for the next, all while we still fell, and I took on the last.

As our backs hit the solid ground with a grunt, the demons were dead. The blackness around us evaporated into nothing. The first thing that hit me was the heat; the next I noticed was the dirt-covered ground since a few jagged rocks pushed into my back and butt.

Groaning, I rolled to the side to find Thorn slowly sitting up.

I did the same, wincing from the pain in my back, chest, and ass. Glancing around, I took in the street we'd landed in.

Wait… Hell had streets?

My eyes widened; shock radiated throughout me. It

seemed Hell had more than just streets. Hell looked a lot like Vegas. In the distance, there were lights flashing, music played, and I sensed the magic surrounding the city.

All in Hell.

Thorn and I were in the desert part of Vegas Hell. The heat beat down on me. I hated blistering warm days. I shielded my eyes and looked up into the sunny sky. Was all of this magic? An illusion? It couldn't be because I could only sense the magic coming from the city area.

Glancing back to Thorn, I said, "Paige is going to kill us."

He snorted out a laugh and stood, his hands going to his waist while he stretched. "Christ, you're right. So we'd better find a way back to her quickly."

Standing, I brushed at my clothes. "I have a feeling we'll find the only way back in that place." I pointed to the city. He looked behind him and cursed.

"Are we really going into a city full of demons?" he asked.

"We'll have to."

He cursed again. "For Paige," he said.

I nodded. "For Paige. Hey, maybe Lucifer will be in there somewhere and take us with him since he wants to see Paige soon anyway."

Thorn slapped me on the back as I stopped beside him. "Your optimism is outstanding." I shrugged. He added, "Great fighting back there."

I knew my cheeks were warmer than just from the sun; I didn't do well with compliments. "I didn't do much."

He scoffed and slung his arm around my shoulders, as if he'd done it a million times before. We started walking before he said, "Not much… yeah, we'll go with that."

"Your fighting skills are... ah, amazing." Which they were.

He glanced down at me and smiled. "Thanks." He released his arm from around me. "You ready to jog?"

I hated jogging. "Sure." I nodded as my lips thinned. For some reason, Thorn found it amusing and started laughing.

CHAPTER NINE
THORN

Alex glanced at me again, after we'd been running for a little while, and after I'd kept him from tripping about five times. His good mood and optimism seemed long gone since he was scowling around the area. Finally, he got up the courage to ask, "Why are you smiling? We had our asses handed to us. Grace, with an extra boost of blood magic, is probably on the way back to the community to harm Paige. Selma is still God knows where. Your men weren't even there. We're stuck in Hell, running into a city where there will be millions of demons who would take great pleasure in killing us."

"We're alive. We fought well together. Paige will be protected with Asher and Nate. Plus, there're all the people she's charmed, even in the short amount of time she's been there. Selma will reappear, and we'll take care of her then." My smile faded. "My men did their duty. They knew, like I did, what would be involved. Battles can be lost. It saddens me deeply this was one of them, and when we get home, I'll grieve with the rest of my men for their losses. Now isn't the time."

"I'm sorry," he blurted, and I knew he meant it. I could hear it and see it in his frown and furrowed brows.

Alex hadn't meant it. He'd spoken without thinking, and I reacted. Their loss sat in my gut, churning painfully, but I had to push it aside. I had to think positive because it all counted to help us get home. So I offered him a smile—it was weak, but there—and he returned one just as weak.

I went on answering his concerns. "We may be in Hell, but Lucifer does want to meet Paige, and hopefully he wants an ally in her, so maybe he'll keep us safe. We may have to fight again, but I'm confident in our skills."

He harrumphed, unsure of my words, but I believed them. Alex was a powerful mage, one who kicked ass against three witches and demons easily, without even breaking into a sweat. I was glad he was on our side. If it wasn't for the blood magic he seemed fearful of, then we would have walked out of that place.

"Who do you think that other demon was?" he asked, helping me push away the mournful thoughts of losing my men by changing the subject. I valued him for it. Alex was slightly puffing and sweating from jogging. We were miles away from the city, though, and I wondered if he'd make it. I would mention to Nate to up Alex's physical activities. He caught me looking at him since I hadn't answered him; he glared, but his cheeks were pink. "If I wasn't sure they'd sense me using my magic, I'd transport us or float all the way there."

Yep, he needed to not rely on his powers, something he might be realizing since he was suffering from exercise. Although, it had me wondering how his body was so fit when he didn't seem to like to work out.

For now, I'd let it slide. I had a feeling he'd listen to Nate and Asher more than me, until we got to know one another better.

"To answer your question, I think the demon is one who's trying to rise up in ranks here. However, he seemed weak on earth, which was why either he or Grace sought each other out to help one another. Grace probably promised him helpful minions, and in return, he gave her all the power he had to open the portal to Hell. He'd be here rejuvenating his strength somewhere, expecting us to be dragged into his lair. Then Grace would have felt drained opening the portal, which was why she had to use blood magic, in the end, to make sure the portal stayed open long enough to get us here. If we hadn't killed the demons on the way down, they would have delivered us to their master for the reward they were promised. If somehow they managed to get us to him, then right about now, he'd probably be stripping us of our power."

Alex stumbled over some loose rocks again. I caught his arm and found him staring at me in shock. "That sounded really accurate."

I grinned. "I've been in the brotherhood for a very long time. I've learnt how people think and strategize a lot of outcomes before they can even happen. Usually I'm spot on, which was how I became the commander of them all and had an ear to the former queen."

He nodded. "That makes sense."

Asher had spoken to me before about Alex, how he'd been the best in school and sought after from the council for many teams, but Asher had been the first captain to approach him personally. He'd picked their team right after. He'd told me how he was young in mage years, but still had a lot to learn, not in work, but within himself. He wasn't confident of his worth. He was shy around people who interested him, yet he'd grown in the month since Paige had come into our lives.

He interested me like Asher and Nate had.

Our family couldn't have been more perfectly put together than if I'd tried to do so myself.

I was pleased to have him in my life. Pleased and happy to

have the family I now had, and I would do anything to protect them all.

"Can I ask you something?"

"Sure, anything," he answered.

That made me smile, yet I wasn't sure he'd like my line of questions, and it annoyed me to even think of upsetting him. Still, it was something all of us should know about him. "Blood magic, you seemed disgusted by it."

He glanced off to the side and sighed. His eyes returned to in front of him, which was probably good; he wasn't the steadiest on his feet while running. "I've studied it, had a cousin lost to it, but shockingly, I've never had to fight against it."

"You're strong, Alex," I told him.

He shrugged. "My cousin killed his whole family because of it. I've never wanted anything to do with blood magic, but with the life we now have… I'll have to make sure I know everything there is to counter any type of blood magic." He almost looked green from the thought.

"Do you believe you can counter it?"

"I'm not sure, which is what scares me most."

"I'll help you find out somehow."

He shot me a quick look of surprise before tripping, and I had to grab him again. "You will?"

I smiled. "Of course. We're family now. We help each other out."

"Thank you," he mumbled, his cheeks tinting once again.

"Anything at any time, Alex, I'm there."

He bit on his bottom lip, but I saw his grin. "Are you happy with…?"

"Everything that's happened?" He nodded. "Yes. Hell yes. Paige is amazing, perfect really. I wasn't sure we'd all get along; it worried me. I didn't even think any of you liked me. Especially Nate, but how he's claimed me, changed that."

"Nate's prickly. He always has been, and I think he always will be, but that's just him. He's changed a bit since, um, claiming us."

I laughed. "I can tell. He's almost sweet, in a possessive way toward you. I look forward to knowing you all more."

"Same with you, I mean, getting to know you."

I bumped his shoulder. Once again, he tripped, but my arm went out around his waist, steadying him. I gave it a squeeze before letting go as we kept up our steady pace. "The future looks bright, even with everything still to deal with."

He nodded, smiling again. "It does."

My ears picked up on a sound. I grabbed Alex's arm and pulled him to a stop. He looked at me, and I held my finger up to my lips. Even over his heavy breaths, I heard it again—a howl.

I spun back the way we'd come. "Fuck."

"What?" Alex snapped.

"Hellhounds and demons running this way." I glanced down at him. "They've got our scent."

"They're hunting us," he concluded.

I nodded. We both started running again.

"Should we risk me using my magic?"

"Let's save it for our last resort."

"Thorn…."

I glanced at him from over my shoulder; they were gaining on us quickly. "Yeah?"

"I'm not fast, and I won't be able to keep going for much longer," he admitted. Shame shone in his eyes before he looked ahead of us. We were about a mile out. I wasn't sure we'd make it without being caught and either ripped apart—

because there were a lot of those fuckers—or taken to someone who could be stronger than the both of us.

"Sorry," I said.

"What for?" He gasped when I picked him up and flung him over my shoulder. He held on as I changed to ghoul and sped over the terrain—triple the speed of what we'd been running.

"This… is… humiliating," Alex panted. He grabbed the top of my jeans, holding on and trying to steady his bouncing.

"It's not. Keep an eye on them. If they get close, it'll be you saving our asses."

"You… have… a nice one… to save."

It was my turn to almost trip. I righted us and laughed. "Are you seriously checking me out while we're running for our lives?"

"No," he fired back quickly, bringing out another laugh from me. Him admitting that he liked how I looked was something to explore another time—when we weren't running to save ourselves.

After a while, I asked, "How we doing?"

"They're closing in, but we're still far enough away."

"Okay," I clipped. It was good having Alex watching them because all I had to do was concentrate on getting us to the city. Fuck. As we drew close, I caught the bustling city and also the sentries who stood surrounding the place.

There were too many. We couldn't take them all on.

They spotted us. A roar erupted through the thick, warm air. Stopping, I placed Alex on his feet.

"What?" he said, then looked to where I was. I heard his gulp as they raced toward us.

We were surrounded.

"Time to use my magic?" Alex asked.

A snort dropped from my lips unexpectedly. "Yeah. Can you get us in there?"

"I can. We'll just have to see if we'll be detected afterward."

They grew closer.

"Let's do it."

Alex's power rose. His eyes changed to purple, the shade glowing, the air chilling, and yet he waited.

"What are you doing?" I asked anxiously. They were nearly upon us.

"Hold on to me," he said, his voice thicker, deeper.

I wrapped my arms around his waist just as a blast shot out of him and slid over the desert. I witnessed the surrounding army fall to the ground just before light shone around us, and that same feeling of being transported took over me.

I opened my eyes to see we now stood in a small, darkened room. The light under the door shone enough for me to make out we were in a broom closet. "Are you okay?" I asked when Alex stumbled forward after I released him.

"Just weakened a little. Give me a moment. I'll be okay."

"What did you do to them?"

"Put them to sleep. I'm not sure how long they'll stay like that."

My hands slid from his arms up to his shoulders. He lifted his head and blinked up at me. "Alex, there were thousands out there."

He nodded. "I know. I could kill them, but it could have knocked me out. A sleeping spell was easier."

The power he held inside of him was amazing.

I tugged him toward me and kissed him hard. He moaned

under my lips, and I found his tongue to play with my own. Pulling back, I said, "You saved us."

He stared up at me in a bit of a daze. "Don't say that yet. I'm not sure where I've landed us. I just made sure it was a room no one was in." Smiling, I kissed him again. He gently pushed on my chest and muttered, "If you keep doing that, my weakness will continue."

I laughed, and he covered my mouth. Grabbing his hand, I pulled it down to whisper, "I'll go out and scope the area—"

"No. Just give me a moment and we'll go together."

"All right." I pulled him against me again and twisted enough to sit us in the cramped area with him between my legs. He didn't even fight it. He rested back against me and breathed deeply. He sounded asleep, but I knew better. He'd still be alert; he was just trying to gain some energy back.

"Couple more minutes," he mumbled.

"Sure," I whispered.

Laughter and then music started outside the room.

Christ, where the fuck were we and would we have to fight our way out? We needed to find out where Lucifer was. He'd be our best chance to get out of there. Hopefully.

Right then, I wasn't too sure of anything, and I didn't like the thought of Alex having to use his reserves of power. It could harm him more than help.

Usually, I wouldn't let worry seep into my veins, but fuck, with Alex there it did. He was family. He was ours, and I didn't want him to risk himself more. Absently, I massaged the back of his neck since his head was turned into my shoulder.

"We could wait until their party stops," I suggested. "They could be drinking and pass out by the end of it."

"No. They'll sense us soon. I'm blocking our scents and power from them, but I won't be able—"

"Fuck, you shouldn't be doing it. You're trying to get energy back, not waste it."

He chuckled low. "It's not a waste, and it's easy to do." Groaning, he started to move away until I pulled him back. "We have to make a move now. My magic is already building."

"Alex."

He turned in my arms and smiled. "Trust me."

I searched his eyes. Already they looked livelier. "I do."

"Good." He pecked my lips, blushed for doing so, and then quickly stood. "We'll go out there. I'll block our powers, and hopefully they'll think we're new demons or something so we can get out." He wouldn't meet my gaze now. I'd deal with that later, make sure he knew I wanted his lips on mine any time, or else I wouldn't have kissed him before.

"Sounds like a plan."

He nodded, opened the door, and stepped out. I followed quickly. My body buzzed, and I saw we were in some type of living room before I caught his "Motherfuck—" He froze as all eyes were on us. Out of the corner of his mouth, he said, "Seems they blocked my block and knew exactly what we are."

Of fucking course the demons didn't allow anyone to goddamn hide.

They stood from the couches, from the stools at the bench, from the table where they'd sat playing poker. They all stood smiling like they'd just won the lottery.

Only we were their winnings.

The front door in front of us burst open. I stood in a

fighting stance while Alex called his power up. The sunlight blinded us for a moment, and I blinked rapidly.

A long, loud noise sounded throughout the room. The demons, to my utter fucking shock, sank to their knees.

Alex gasped. I swung my gaze back to the doorway, and my mouth dropped open. I couldn't believe it.

CHAPTER TEN
PAIGE

I didn't know how long went by, but eventually, Asher sent a message to Nate telling him he'd taken me down to my sister's suite to get my mind off things. They'd probably only just woken up, but it was a good idea. The kids were always a good distraction.

Especially when Alex and Thorn's emotions inside me were lost. I felt the loss even more since I'd just made the connection and bonded with Alex, but Asher told me they would have blocked the connection for my sake.

I knocked on the door, and it sprang open by a smiling Sophie. She wrapped her arms around me and hugged me close. Lifting her head, she dug her chin into my hip. "Hiya, Aunty Paige."

I ran my hands over her head. "Hiya, Sophie. Is your mom awake?"

"I think so. I didn't call out this morning. I snuck out my room and heard her yell at Daddy about doing something harder."

Oh shit.

Asher choked, holding back a laugh.

"Ah, yeah, okay. I'm sure she'll be out soon."

Asher choked again, and I elbowed him. Curling my arm around Sophie's shoulders, I ushered her back into the living room. "You know you shouldn't answer the door on your own."

"But there's men who watch to keep us safe. Mommy told me."

"I know, honey, but your mom and dad would still like you to never answer the door without them around."

She sighed. "Okay." She skipped over to Asher, her arms already raised. He scooped her up and swung her around, drawing out a giggle. "Hiya, Uncle Asher."

He stilled, just blinking down at her.

"What's wrong with him?" she asked.

I laughed. "Nothing, honey. He's just happy that you're calling him Uncle Asher."

"Oh." She grinned. "Mommy said I could when I asked. And I get to call Nate my uncle Nate, and Thorn my uncle Thorn, and Alex my uncle Alex. Even though Alex does supercool magic and I wanted to marry him, Mommy said I couldn't because he was your boyfriend, Aunty Paige. Then I asked how come you get to date, like, four boys, but she said she'd tell me when I'm older or that I had to ask you… so…?"

I didn't know what to say. What I did think, though, was that I was going to kill my sister for leaving it up to me.

Maybe it would be best for the simple answer. "Because I love them all, and they were made just for me."

"That's amazing!" she cried, and then squished Asher's cheeks together. "Isn't that amazing!" He nodded, smiling, also trying to hold in his laughter again. Sophie didn't. She giggled and announced, "I want to be just like Aunty Paige and love lots of boys."

Oh fuck.

"How about we make a start on breakfast for everyone?" I suggested quickly.

"Yes," she cried. "I'm starving."

Oscar was the next to rise, just as I had the bacon and eggs cooking while Asher talked, and Sophie got the cutlery and cups out. My nephew walked in looking like a little monster himself with his shuffling feet, messy hair, and tired eyes. He made his way straight to Asher and leaned into Asher's side. I looked on, my heart melting as Asher put his arm around Oscar and said, "Morning, buddy." Oscar grunted back in reply.

Asher would have made an amazing father. The only time I saw his expression that soft was when he was with me and the rest of the men. Outside our rooms, he was cold and hard. It was beautiful to see the difference he held, the gentleness to him, for the people important to him. I wished I could give my men children.

Sadness washed through me. I couldn't regret what I'd become or where my life was at because I had my men, but I would have loved to have extended our own little family with their kids.

Asher's gaze lifted, his gates opened, and he flooded me with contentment and happiness. I smiled warmly at him and went back to cooking. No, I could never regret where my life was because I had four beautiful, amazing men. If only Ezra were around…. I shook my head from that thought before it took me under.

"Aunty," Oscar mumbled.

"Yes, little man?"

"Can I have pancakes?"

"You can have anything. As soon as I'm done here, I'll make you some."

"Thanks. Uncle Asher, do you want pancakes?"

I glanced over my shoulder to see Asher's eyes shine, his chest expanding. I could feel how honored he was the kids were calling him uncle.

"Morning," my sister announced, walking in with a satis-fied smile and fresh from the shower, dressed in jeans and a woolen sweater.

"Morning, Mommy," Sophie cried and ran at Yasmin to hug her. "I got up myself this morning, and then Aunty Paige was here. Did Daddy end up doing it harder?"

I laughed and Asher chuckled when Yasmin choked on her own saliva. "W-What?"

"I got up without calling out like you asked, and I heard you yell at Daddy about doing it harder."

"Ah, right…." Yasmin looked at us for help. We were too busy enjoying her embarrassment.

"It's all right, Soph," Eric said as he walked in. "I took care of it."

"Goodie," she yelled, and then went back to grabbing juice out of the refrigerator.

"Eric," Yasmin whispered in a harsh tone.

"She doesn't know any better."

"But others do." She gestured her head toward us.

Eric just smiled and called "Morning," before he planted a quick kiss on Yasmin's cheek and walked our way.

I froze when a frantic knock sounded on the door. Asher was up out of his seat and at the door in seconds, opening it. He stepped back, and Aggie, the witch who was spying on her coven mistress, moved in. Her eyes wide with worry.

"Eric, take this," I said, handing him the spatula. "Ollie wants pancakes."

"So does Asher," Oscar said quickly.

"I'll let your mom know if we can make it back in time."

He grumbled, "Fine." I gave him a quick kiss on the cheek, then Sophie and finally Yasmin. Only when I went to pull away from my sister, she took my hand. Our eyes met and she studied me.

"I'm okay," I told her.

"Promise?"

I nodded. "I will be. Alex and Thorn went on a mission. I'm just... jittery without them."

She gave me a soft smile. "They'll be okay."

"My queen, please," Aggie called.

My heart lurched. Whatever she had to say was important. Yasmin squeezed my hand. "Go. Be safe."

"I will." With a quick fierce hug, we parted, and I rushed to the door. Asher slipped out first, then me and Aggie. Felnick already stood there with six other guards waiting for an order.

"Down to the office. Felnick, call in more guards because you're in with us. I want four guards to stay here with my family," I told him.

"Yes, my queen." He dropped behind to organize the men while we kept going until we reached my office.

Once inside with the door closed, I went behind the desk and faced Aggie, demanding, "What's wrong?"

"Grace didn't come back last night," Aggie said, ringing her hands together in front of her while Asher slowly moved around to my back. Aggie went on, "She told us she had to head into the city to get more herbs. Something she'd done in the past, but she never came back. I overheard two of her close friends say they hoped her plan goes well. I don't have a good feeling."

The door banged open, and Felnick entered with Alma in his arms.

"Alma," I cried and rushed around the desk, only to have her grin over at me.

"Put me down, handsome. Maybe next time we can do a different kind of riding?" Alma winked up at him while he blushed and set her on her feet.

"What's going on?" I asked, stopping at her side and taking her arm to lead her over to the chair.

She patted my hand with her free one. "Don't fret. I'm fine. Just exhausted from all the darn stairs in here. May I suggest getting elevators?"

"Noted." Asher grinned.

"Good."

"Miss Alma, you said it was urgent to get here, which was why you asked me to carry you," Felnick said.

"Oh yes." She smiled. "I've seen it. The council will soon know of our existence. War is coming. How you choose to approach it will decide on the outcome."

"Can't you just tell us what way to approach it?" I asked.

"No, dear. The powers that be won't let me."

"Can you tell us when at least?" Asher questioned.

"Nope."

"But it must be soon since you've told us now," I said, more to myself than anyone.

Alma smiled up at me as I leaned my butt against the desk in front of her.

"Soon could mean anything. Days, weeks, or even a month," Felnick added. I glanced to him and caught him looking away from Aggie quickly. She didn't see his hungry gaze as her eyes were on the floor.

Until she lifted them and said, "I could go there. Pretend—"

"No." I shook my head. "What you're already doing for us is a risk. I won't have you attempting a bigger one."

"But—"

"No" was clipped. At first, I thought it was Asher. I turned to him, but he shook his head. I glanced to Felnick, who stood with his fists clenched, his jaw locked, and glaring at Aggie like he would kidnap her to protect her.

"I can do whatever I wish, Felnick."

"Oooh, this is good." Alma clapped.

"You cannot when you are so willing to risk your own life all the time."

Aggie's hands dropped to her hips, and her chin lifted in defiance. "Who are you to tell me?"

Felnick's teeth ground together before he bit out, "You'll find out exactly when you're older."

Aggie snorted. "That makes no sense. I'm old enough to know now."

Oh, this was awkward because she totally wasn't getting his point. He wanted her in a naked way. He wanted her in a way he had a say in her future and decisions.

"Fine. You want to know who I am to tell you why I won't allow you to risk your life?"

"Yes."

"Right now? Here in front of everyone?"

Her head jerked back. Confusion washed over her features, dipping her brows and pinching her lips. She opened her mouth, closed it and then opened it again to stutter, "Y-Yes, um, at least, I think so." She glanced at me. "Do I?"

"Yes, you do," Alma said.

Aggie nodded down at her. "Okay." She looked back at Felnick. "Then yes, I want to know."

"I'll be the man in your future, Aggie. I'll be the one in your bed, claiming you as mine, and you'll be the woman who will want to stay there and not risk her life because you'll see a future with me."

Wow, that was awesome.

Aggie's cheeks shot to a deep red. "Uh… no."

Felnick blanched. "No?"

Alma scoffed. "Oh, don't you pretend you don't like him. You've been crushing on him since you were a youngin' I heard."

"Alma!" Aggie yelled.

Felnick was now looking smug. "We'll talk more about this later then."

"I…. What…?" She shook her head. "No, we won't." She glared.

"We'll see." He faced me. "My queen, your guards will be ready for when the time comes for war. I'll even ask around to see if there are others willing to join the fight."

Alma gurgled. We all looked to her; she shook her head.

My brows drew down. "No to others joining?" I asked. She winked. "But war is coming here, we'll need all the people there are if what I hear about the ruthless council is right."

Alma shook her head but said nothing. Obviously, she couldn't speak on the matter.

"Alma," Asher called. She gazed up at him. "Is the war coming here?"

She winked. That was a yes.

"We're missing something," I stated. Alma touched her nose.

"The council will come for us?" Aggie asked.

Alma winked.

"If they come here, will we win?" Asher asked quietly. She shook her head.

"Which is why we don't need more guards," I said quietly. "They'll win no matter." Alma winked, then gurgled, but I was lost in the fear. It was like an invisible fist surrounded my heart and squeezed it tightly. I couldn't lose anyone. The people, *my* people, we had to get them out. Oh God, my family. The kids. All the children.

The door opened and Nate strolled in. "Alma, do we have a chance if we take the fight to them?" He'd been listening at the door.

When Alma lifted her hand and shook it side to side, I knew it meant it was a possibility. It still meant risking my men, my guards. It meant there would be a war with only a slight chance we'd win. But if we didn't take it there, go to them, we didn't have a chance at all.

"I don't fucking like this," Nate announced.

Everyone nodded, looking dejected.

"At least there's a better chance for us if we go there, or we'll risk losing our lives and the people under our care," Felnick said. We could all hear the tension in his voice, the worry.

I dropped to my knees and grabbed Alma's hands. "Can we run? Can the mages and witches move our community someplace else?"

She shook her head. "The fight is inevitable."

"Meaning even if we move, it'll still happen in the future," Nate said.

Asher's hands landed on my shoulders. Softly, he said, "You knew this would come, love."

I bit my bottom lip and nodded. I straightened and turned into him, gripping his T-shirt. "I just didn't know it would be so soon. It kills me knowing you will all walk into danger with me."

"If we don't, the council could ruin so many more lives. They've killed innocents, probably kidnapped some more.

They need to be stopped, and we're the best chance to do it."
Nate told me things I already knew; it didn't mean the mind-numbing fear would ease.

Asher tucked my hair behind my ear. "Take that fear and switch it to anger when the time comes."

I wished I could walk into the battle on my own. However, I wasn't stupid. For the people, I would have a better chance of protecting their future with my men and whoever would be willing to go with us at my side.

"I will," I told him, because I knew I would.

CHAPTER ELEVEN
ASHER

She was amazing.

I could feel her terror, but I knew without a doubt she would do what she had to for the future. To make sure the people she protected were safe from the clutches of the council. We all knew there would come a time we'd have to do something about the council members and had hoped it wouldn't be for a while, but fate had stepped up our timeline.

Looking to Nate, I saw the resolve in his eyes. When the time did come, we would do everything to make sure our mate would live on for a happier time within the supernatural world.

"For now, and until Alex and Thorn are back, maybe we should get back on the subject of Grace," I suggested.

"Ah, yes, Grace," Alma murmured.

An explosion erupted outside.

I flashed to the window and peered out, sensing Nate at my side. We both took in the chaos. People were scattered below, running away from the huge hole in the gate.

"I knew there was something else I forgot to tell you," Alma said.

"What?" Paige demanded.

Alma sighed. I glanced back to see her studying her nails. "It seems Grace has taken to the dark side, Obi-Wan. She's come to kill you using blood magic." Another explosion rocked the castle. "Better get out there before she takes her anger out on innocent bystanders."

Nate tugged his shirt from his body, and Paige yelled harshly, "Look away, Aggie."

"I've got it," Felnick said, crossing the room quickly to cover Aggie's eyes.

Nate snorted and removed his pants. "Open the door for me, Paige, and stay here."

The queen called for her power. Her eyes changed, her claws extending along with her teeth. "You are not leaving me behind. Neither of you are," she snarled, looking from Nate to me, and when I nodded, she then glanced back to Nate.

He cursed yet didn't fight with her any longer. The shift came over him. His body morphed, bones popped, and in seconds, he landed on all fours as his huge wolf form.

"Felnick, stay here with them," Paige ordered, her hand on the door handle.

"But—"

"Felnick. Alma and Aggie are important to me. Actually, take them to my family's suite and guard all of them."

Felnick tipped his chin down. "Yes, my queen."

She swung the door open, and Nate bounded out before Paige ran into the hall. I quickly followed, the air surrounding me fluttering papers from the desk around the room. I caught Alma's laugh. Together, we raced down the busy hall of people scattering for safety. However, some stopped to watch in awe to see the queen herself running into the threat.

It wasn't that long ago her fear had control. Looking at her now, I would have thought nothing could scare her. Her people, our people, should be proud of the type of queen Paige was.

Along the trek, twenty or so guards joined our line of

defense, but already I could hear the fighting had started outside. I locked my emotions away from my mate. She glanced at me and nodded, then did the same. We couldn't be distracted.

Just as we reached the front door that led into the market area, we heard, "Come out, little queen. It's time to test your strength."

Guards pushed the doors open. We stepped out together. Grace had brought demons along with her. It was those the guards had been fighting while Grace stood just inside the gate and stared on smiling.

Any time someone approached her, they sank to their knees and cried out in pain. She'd protected herself with a spell.

"Ah, there she is. Welcome to the party, little queen." The fighting around us stopped. Everyone, even the demons, watched as Paige walked on slowly, taking in everything.

"I'm just happy you're calling me queen at all, Grace. It means you do see me as one."

Grace's upper lip rose. "You may be queen for now, but I'll rip your powers from your body when I take your heart."

The wolf gnashed his teeth and snarled at Grace even as demons roared and stamped their hooves or feet into the ground.

Paige threw her head back and laughed.

I saw the way Grace's features blanked, her confidence lessened all for a second before a scowl marred her face. "I wouldn't laugh, little queen. My army and I have you outnumbered."

"Take out the main player and the army will fall," I said.

Grace's gaze flicked to me. "You don't stand a chance, vampire."

I shrugged. "We shall see."

She cackled and looked back to Paige. Grace's confidence had her pulling her shoulders back, had a smirk lifting her lips, and an evil glint shining in her eyes. "Tell me something, little queen. Where are your two other men?"

Paige's steps faltered until she stopped completely. "What are you saying, Grace?"

"I heard they went on a mission. I heard they were ambushed. I heard they were taken out." Her smirk grew into a smile.

"What did you do?" Paige demanded, her voice deeper, darker. Her ghoul side would be after vengeance. Fury leaked through her block, but before she could act, we needed answers first. When I took her hand in mine, she gripped me hard, but I knew she'd understand I was just trying to help her. Like the wolf was by stepping in front of her and pressing his body against her legs.

"They're dead."

"You lie," Paige bellowed. She managed a step forward even with the wolf and me holding her.

Grace leaned forward a little. "I don't."

"Do you forget bonded mates can feel when the other has passed?" I question.

Grace's lips thinned. Then she threw her hands out as if to say it didn't matter. "I'm unsure if she'd feel it when they're in Hell."

Fuck.

Even I wasn't sure of the consequences, and when Paige glanced at me, she saw it on my face. Her jaw clenched, her body tensing.

In a low, hard voice, she asked, "And *you* were a part of their ambush?"

Grace, sensing her mistake, took a step back but then stopped.

"Is this how you got more power? Why you switched to using blood magic? You aided the demons?" a voice called from behind us.

"Aggie, Jesus Christ, get the fuck back," Felnick hissed. He'd left Paige's family suite, had disregarded Paige's orders. Even though he did it for the woman he saw as his, he would pay for not listening.

"Ah, sweet Aggie. Come here, dear."

"So you can drain my powers? Where's Montana? Where's Renee?"

Grace didn't answer, and as Aggie stepped up to my side with Felnick at her back, I caught the tears in her eyes. "Even though they followed you blindly, they didn't deserve death just so you can darken your soul."

"Felnick?" Paige snapped low.

"They're safe. The guards are with them. Michael is there with some shifters. Alma sent me after Aggie." When Paige nodded, Felnick relaxed a little, until Aggie took another step forward.

"Now isn't the time to step up, Aggie. I will bury you." Grace stretched her arms out, lifting her hands, and then black smoke swirled. "I will suck the life right out of you, child."

"I'd like to see you try," Aggie clipped.

"Aggie," Felnick snapped. He wrapped his arms around her to pull her back. She stood on his foot, elbowed him in the ribs, and shot off a beam of white light toward Grace.

"Attack," Grace yelled.

Mayhem broke out. The demons attacked anyone they were close to. It was time to let my vampire loose. Especially when my dead heart nearly jumped in my throat when Paige bounded over her wolf and charged the demons who'd surrounded a bear shifter.

Jesus, she would be the death of me.

* * *

PAIGE

As I charged the demons, who were all around a lone bear shifter, fury washed through me. I jumped Nate and raced the bear's way. Out of the corner of my eye, I caught Asher's vampire side bursting out of him. A wave of arousal had my nipples hardening, my clit throbbing, and my body humming.

Now isn't the damn time, body.

In their normal state, my mates turned me into a puddle of desire, but when I saw their monster, it was as if my monster readied my body to take my men. Even in the middle of a fight apparently.

Shaking my head, I pushed off the ground with my feet and landed onto the back of one demon. My arms flung over his enormous hunched shoulders, and I easily slid my claws into his chest. He howled, bucked, and tried to grab me. I locked my legs around his waist and shredded his heart inside his body. The demon dropped to the ground on his knees. I pushed off him, taking his head with me.

I glanced up to see Asher. His green eyes were trained on me, the other demons around the injured bear shifter were on the dirt. All headless. Black blood dripped from Asher's claws.

He was ferocious and amazing to look at.

"Take him inside for help," I told Asher.

He snarled at me. "No. Protect *Mine*." He wanted to stay at my side.

"Please, Asher."

A demon got close to him. Asher's hand snapped out in a blurred movement, and the demon was missing his head.

"No," he demanded.

"It's all right, my queen," Clyde said, appearing out of nowhere. "I'll take care of the shifter. Keep Asher at your side."

"Witches," someone yelled.

"Aggie?" I called, glancing at her, and found her floating in the sky with a bubble surrounding her body as she tried to fight every spell Grace threw at her. Sweat covered her face, worrying me. She could run out of steam before taking Grace down. We had to help.

"They're with her," Aggie said through clenched teeth. Felnick stood below Aggie, moving this way and that with his sword raised high and slicing anything that got too close.

"Fuck," I bit out.

A whimper caught my attention. Nate. I searched around me, knowing he wouldn't be far, and he wasn't. Only what I saw had a haze of anger washing over me. A witch stood over him. Her lips moved, spelling him in some way. Yet he still tried to attack; he crawled toward her on his belly.

"Asher," I called.

"Yes?"

"It's time to feed," I told him.

"The witches," he hissed. Then he curled his arm around my waist. Wind whipped me in the face as he flashed us close to Nate. Asher's hands went to my waist right before he threw me at the bitch attacking Nate.

Shock crossed her features as I crashed into her. She landed on her back on the ground. I rolled to break my fall, and then on all fours, I crawled back to her. Her hands glowed, but all I wanted was her death. Nothing else worried me. She'd hurt what was mine. She would pay.

As I pushed her shoulders in the ground, I ignored the burning sensation at my waist and dropped my mouth to her neck where I bit. My razor-sharp teeth easily slid into her soft skin. I tore out a chunk, spat it to the side, and then went in for more. She screamed, wiggled, and fought, but it wouldn't be enough.

More screams of terror sounded around me before they were cut off and I felt the thump of something hitting the ground. Asher was at work.

Nate was at my side, growling. Even though I ate at her neck, she still managed another loud yell, and then I saw Nate get a hold of one of her arms in his mouth. The pain at my waist disappeared as I heard her take her last breath.

Lifting off her, I pushed my claws into her chest, cutting through her ribs and grabbing her heart, crushing it into nothing.

Nate whimpered at my side as he shoved his nose against my waist. I sat back and lifted my top. Two handprints were burned into my skin, near down to the bone.

Nate licked at my face as I ran my hands through his hair. "I'll be fine. It's already healing."

"You will not best me," Grace bellowed.

Asher stopped at my side and slowly helped me up, and we watched Grace take a step closer to Aggie before she threw a black ball of something at her. It surrounded Aggie's bubble.

"Shit," I whispered, seeing the bubble slowly being eaten away.

Aggie cried out in frustration. Her hands shot out—white light built in each palm. Her eyes slid to mine, and then in my mind, I heard her voice. *"Her defenses will be down for only a second. You'll need to get to her and kill her."*

Clenching my jaw, I nodded.

Taking Asher's hand in mine, I whispered, "Get ready."

"I heard." Aggie must have told all of us.

Around us, the guards still fought the dwindling demons and what was left of the witches. I saw Clyde drinking from one witch, and the bear shifter was up and back to fighting, even when I'd thought he'd be out of action for a while.

A howl swept over the area. Nate lifted his head and joined in.

The wolves were on the way, and close. As I looked toward the gate, I saw the first few race through, attacking where they could. Helping.

Quickly, I moved my gaze back to Aggie just as the last of Grace's spell consumed Aggie's bubble.

"No!" Felnick bellowed as the blackness reached out for Aggie, latching onto her foot.

Her eyes slid to us then back again.

This was it.

CHAPTER TWELVE
PAIGE

My heart gave a fearful hard thump, but I had to steel it. I had to push it back. For the people. For Aggie and for us.

The blackness slid up Aggie's body, but it was as if she ignored it; however, I could see how hard she gritted her teeth. Aggie's whole body went into the push of her power as she flung her hands forward and shot two orbs of white light at Grace.

It surrounded Grace's own invisible bubble. Grace gasped as her barrier started to get devoured.

Asher's arm shot around my waist. He flashed us forward as a gap appeared in the bubble. I felt his hesitancy in what he knew he had to do. "Do it," I clipped. He did. Asher threw me through the gap. I rolled, pushed up, and jammed my fist into Grace's stomach. Blood sprayed. I gripped the flesh and organs inside her.

She let out a noise, glanced down, and gripped my wrist. Grace looked up and then smiled. But before she could get cocky, Nate was inside the bubble. He jumped onto her back and latched his powerful jaw around the back of her neck.

Fire from her hands burned my skin. I clamped my lips closed so I didn't scream. The scent near had me gagging. Nate whimpered. His whole body shook like he was being shocked over and over. He dropped to the ground.

Slowly, I glanced up. "You'll pay for that."

"I don't think—"

A screech of pain had me turning my head to see a lifeless Aggie fall out of the sky. Felnick managed to catch her and lay her gently to the ground. His hands slid over her, and when he looked up with pain-filled eyes, I knew she wasn't alive.

I wanted to cry, to let the anguish consume me, but I couldn't.

Grace, in the distraction, managed to push my hand out of her. She laughed maniacally as her body healed quicker than any creature before.

"Poor, poor Aggie. She was no match for blood magic. Just like you won't be."

My wrist still burned, but I straightened and then smiled. "That's the problem. I'm never alone."

Asher's hands wrapped around her chest, his claws digging in between her breasts. A bout of jealousy had my upper lip raising and growling. My vampire smirked until blackness—the same stuff that killed Aggie—burst from Grace's hands.

Asher laughed. He leaned down and said, "Blood magic does nothing to me, fool. I'm made of darkness and blood."

He stabbed his claws inside her and peeled her chest and ribs open with ease. Grace's hands dropped, her eyes blinking sluggishly, her body slowly dying. The only thing that kept her heart beating, which I could clearly see, was the dark magic.

I stepped up to her.

"I am queen. I am the *ghoul* queen. I was meant to rule over all races. I was meant to change the ways. I revel in the knowledge you'll die knowing you failed. To me, to Aggie, to the shifters, and my people because you are weak and contaminated."

I thrust my hand into her open chest and pulled out her heart. I lifted it to my mouth as the life in her eyes faded and bit into it as it beat for the last time.

The remaining demons vanished into the air, the last witch standing, who fought on Grace's side, turned her glowing hand on herself, and her body fell to the ground. A guard bent to check her vitals. He smiled over at me. She'd killed herself so she didn't have to face our wrath.

I looked back at Asher. He let her body drop to the floor while his green glowing eyes devoured me. He'd never be fazed by what I did, how I was. In fact, if the bulge in his pants was anything to go by, he enjoyed seeing my monster as much as I did his.

Something nudged my thigh. I threw the heart to the ground and looked down. Nate sat there and rubbed his head into my thigh. I crouched and wrapped my arms around his neck, taking his scent into my dead lungs. He licked my face, even though his dark eyes told me he was pissed about something.

Standing, I gripped his fur and took a step toward Asher, using the back of my arm to wipe away the blood around my mouth. I needed my men. Both of them.

"My queen."

Pausing, I turned my head to see Felnick there.

The fog from my men lifted and I remembered.

Oh God, Aggie.

"Aggie," I whispered, ready to run to her side. Until Felnick's hand shot up.

"My queen." He bowed his head. "I couldn't save her. I failed her."

Over his shoulder, I saw Clyde picking up Aggie in his arms.

"What's going on?"

"He was willing to save her."

"He changed her?"

"Yes." Sadness overtook his eyes. "I didn't have a choice."

"It doesn't mean she won't be yours," Asher said, his vampire side no longer around.

"She'll have a bond with her master—"

"If it's meant to be, no bond with the master can change it."

"Felnick," Clyde called. "Come with us. She'll need you too."

Felnick's eyes widened, surprised. He'd honestly thought he'd lost any chance he had with Aggie. Felnick had been scared Clyde wouldn't want him around his new addition into his clan.

"My queen," Felnick said, though he didn't look back at me.

"Go. Be with her," I told him.

He took off, stopping at Clyde's side to take her hand in his. Clyde said something. Felnick looked up in shock, his lips thinning, but then tipped up before he nodded.

"What was that about?" I asked.

"Clyde has offered for Felnick to stay in his place and for her to feed upon him first."

I dipped my brows in confusion. "Isn't Felnick a ghoul? Does he have the blood to fill her?"

"Do you bleed, love?"

I glanced down to my arm to my tee where blood stained it from my wounds. "Yes, but I have a beating heart."

"That is true, but there will be enough blood in Felnick to supply Aggie with what she needs before he will have to feed to replenish the blood drained from his body."

Oh, I got it now. The blood from our kills stayed in our body, which was why my people bled without a beating heart.

Honestly, I still had a lot more learning to do.

Since arriving, each day seemed to have spun by in a blur of activity. The only moments that took their time was when I was with my men. Even still, they weren't long enough. I couldn't wait for the day where I had nothing to do but lounge around. If it ever came.

"Will Aggie be all right? Does... I mean, she'll still be a witch, right?"

Asher nodded. "She will, love. She'll be a hybrid. Half witch, half vampire."

"Are there many hybrids?" Seemed strange since there'd been many rules about cross mating and such.

"No. She'll be the first here. At least that I've sensed so far."

That made more sense.

"My queen" was voiced from our side. I turned to see a man who was even bigger built than Nate.

"Yes?"

He dropped to his knees and bowed, his forehead nearly touching the dirt. "Thank you for your assistance in saving me."

He had to be the bear shifter.

"You're welcome..."

"Leon Walton, my queen."

"Please stand," I asked. He did and towered over me, though that seemed normal around here. "Are you a part of Thorn's brotherhood?"

A pang of loss cracked my chest.

No. I ground my teeth together. They weren't lost. They were alive, and I would get them back.

"No, my queen. I'm a mere shifter. We don't belong with the brotherhood."

I scoffed; I couldn't help it. It seemed Thorn had to fold within the old laws as well. I knew he wouldn't have been discriminating on purpose; he would have followed the orders of the old advisers or queen.

Upon my scoff, Leon's gaze snapped up from the ground to meet mine. Asher and Nate rumbled out a growl. I fisted my hand in Nate's fur and took Asher's hand.

"It's all right." I lifted my chin and addressed Leon, "You were willing to fight for the people without even being a part of the brotherhood. Your courage is amazing. If you would, I'd like to invite you and four others you trust completely to safeguard my own family. But you will also be working together with another four brotherhood guards, if you accept."

He closed his eyes and dropped his chin. "What you bestow upon me is the biggest honor. Members of my sleuth would protect your family with our lives."

Dropping Asher's hand, I reached out for Leon's, only Asher, with his glowing eyes and descended fangs, grabbed my hand back and pulled it to his side. His grip unwavering as he hissed at Leon.

Leon tipped his head to the side, his lips twitching. "She is your mate, vampire."

"We're a little out of sorts after everything," I told Leon.

"Of course."

"How many are in your sleuth?"

"I have eight brothers, a sister and her mate, and they have four children."

Wow, okay, that was a lot of siblings.

"My queen," Gregory said, stopping at our side.

"Gregory." I smiled. "What are you doing here?"

"Jessup," he said simply.

"Yes, please thank him and his pack for his assistance."

"It was the least we could do," Jessup called, walking up to our huddle.

"How are you healed already?"

I was surprised when Jessup and Gregory blushed. Nate at my side snorted. Even in wolf form he still managed to do that.

"Ah…." Jessup rubbed the back of his neck. His naked neck. On his naked body. "I shifted, and a mate can, ah, help the healing process after."

"You're naked," I pointed out in case he didn't already know.

He chuckled. "Comes with the territory of being a shifter. We don't care about nudity."

I glanced down at Nate. I jabbed my finger on my chest and then down at him. "We care about it. You don't go around naked in front of anyone."

He huffed, not liking being told what to do.

"How are you not naked?" I asked Leon, noting he wore jeans and a flannel shirt.

He grinned. "My sleuth and I leave clothes all over the place. Seems my sister doesn't want to see us naked, and her mate doesn't want anyone looking at her naked either."

"I think I'll like them. That's what you should do…. Not saying that naked isn't fine. Anyone who wants to go around naked can. Being naked for some is natural—"

"Love, how about you stop saying naked?"

"Good idea." I nodded. "Jessup, thank you and your pack for helping. Gregory, could I please ask a favor?"

"Of course, my queen."

"Are you able to set up some rooms for Leon?"

"Oh no, my queen," Leon said. "Please and thank you for the kind offer, but we live in the village, and we'd like to stay there. Our cubs go to the school there. We'd need to stay close. Since there are eight brothers of mine, we can rotate shifts to attend your family. Four on four off and so on, if you wouldn't mind." He dipped his head.

"Leon, that's fine, but as long as I'm not taking you away from any jobs you have in the village. I didn't even think of it before."

"Our jobs will be replaced by another easily. Nothing to worry about. It is honestly an honor to work for the queen."

I bit my bottom lip, feeling guilty for taking them away from the village, from their sleuth.

"Please, my queen. We would be looked upon as well-respected individuals if you allow us to still have the jobs to guard your family."

"As long as everyone in your, um, sleuth is okay with it."

His smile took up half his face. "They will be, but if you'll excuse me, I'll go and speak with them now."

I nodded. "All right, thank you."

"No, my queen, thank you again. My brothers would have been here, but they were far away fishing. They should return soon, and then I'll have your answer, which I'm sure will be a yes."

"Okay, Leon. If I'm not available, please let Gregory or Eric know, and they'll inform me."

He bowed, turned, and raced off.

"Your kindness has made that man's day, and no doubt his

family's. Shifters have never been sought after from a queen, until now." Jessup smiled.

I glanced down at Nate. My fingers sifted through his fur on his shoulder. "Shifters were never a lesser being. We're all equal."

"But it is those who see it that makes a tremendous queen, such as yourself," Jessup said.

I shrugged. Asher chuckled. "Our mate doesn't do well with compliments."

I glared up at him. "No, I don't. Can we start cleaning up around here. I could use a shower. If only Alex was...." Misery twisted my stomach. I gripped Nate tighter to me and told Asher, "They're alive."

"I'm sure they are, love."

"They are." They had to be.

He nodded. "You would know, my love."

"I would, and I know they're alive. They'll come back. They'll... they're in Hell, Asher. Hell." I spun to Gregory. "I need to call Lucifer. Get me on the phone to Lucifer. Now."

His gaze dimmed. "I'm sorry, my queen, we have no way of contacting him."

"But he called me."

"I heard he had, but he wouldn't make it traceable. The former queen never had a number to contact him. If the devil wants to see you, *he* shows, *he* calls, never the other way around."

Frustration had me throwing my head back and yelling. How was this fair?

"They're in Hell, Asher. Can they survive Hell?"

"They would do anything to come back to you, my love. Anything."

Nate whimpered at my side and pressed himself into me. My insides were a swirling pool of fear, worry, and misery.

"Take the queen inside. We'll take care of this mess," Jessup offered.

"No!" I shouted, then took a deep breath. "I need to keep busy. I need something to do."

Asher nodded, and Nate started to move off. "Nate," I called and he turned. "I-I'd like you here with me." I couldn't let them out of my sight. Not now.

He barked, only I didn't talk wolf.

"I believe he's going to get dressed so no one here sees him naked," Jessup offered.

"Right, well, that's good." I nodded and then shot Nate a thumbs-up. I was sure I saw him roll his eyes at the gesture before leaving.

My gaze drifted down to Grace. I wished she wasn't dead already. Just thinking of what Thorn and Alex were going through in Hell made me want to kill her again and again.

They had to be alive.

No, they were. Deep inside me, I would have felt their loss, and even when their links to me were blocked, I would still know.

I would.

CHAPTER THIRTEEN
PAIGE

I stood back and eyed my work. I screwed my nose up. What had I been thinking painting Alex's room in purple? I tried to get the same color to match his eyes, but now it just looked like a squished eggplant. However, I wasn't the best painter. Thorn's room could contest to that when I'd messed up his walls, and maybe I got some on his floor and bed, in a deep red.

"We have to do something," Nate mock whispered to Asher behind me.

Asher hummed. I didn't know if he was agreeing or disagreeing.

Okay, maybe I might have lost my mind a little. The wolf pack wouldn't have me back until I fixed their plumbing. Something I'd tried to help with since I'd been human not that long ago, compared to them at least. But now their water only ran cold water. Thankfully, Leon's brother had experience in plumbing, but he was still working on the other problem I'd made.

People around the castle stepped out of my way these days since I'd stopped everyone I passed and asked them if I could help with anything. With a few mistakes with sewing, cooking, gardening, and home renovations, they learned to dodge me, so they wouldn't feel guilty and have to accept my help. At least they'd gotten over the queen asking to assist people.

And that was only because my rant about how queens were able to do whatever they wanted in a time of need and support, or anytime for that matter, had been spread when the first person questioned why the queen would sink so low as to do mundane things.

It had been two weeks since Grace had come in ready for a battle and informed me that Alex and Nate were in Hell.

Two weeks.

Two long-ass, frustrating weeks.

Every minute that passed, I made sure I kept busy, else I'd be a mess in the corner of a room, holding a dolly and asking for my mommy.

Nate growled in the back of his throat. "You know they're alive or else we would both know it. Our souls would have lost a part of itself."

I knew they were. *We* knew they were since Nate had claimed them both and had made his own connection to them. We just never ventured to the part where we were unsure. Would we feel the broken bond even from Hell?

I quickly pushed that thought away and went over to the paint tin. "I know," I muttered.

"Paige, you need to rest. You've only had a few hours sleep in two weeks, and you need to feed," Asher said. "Your people are concerned about you."

"You also look like shit," Nate added.

Straightening, I swung my eyes his way and lasered him with a glare.

His brows raised. "You do." He walked to the door and opened it. I saw Gregory standing there. "Make her a meal, normal food and flesh. Bring it up but leave it outside the door. Have a guard watch it."

Gregory smiled, and he dipped his head before walking

off. Nate closed the door and turned, crossing his arms over his chest. "You need a shower, rest, and food before this fucking meeting tomorrow, and I'm going to make sure you get all three."

I snorted, rolled my eyes, and picked my brush up to walk back to the wall. He was right. I knew he was. I should have wanted to look my best for the ceremony in front of all to swear Aggie, Leon, and his brothers into my close fold; however, I just couldn't bring myself out of this depressed state of worry to care enough. I was also concerned that if I slept, I would dream. Even though I hadn't had that dream I used to have since I'd been there, I had no doubt my mind would twist and show me Alex and Thorn dead. I couldn't handle it.

I was beyond pissed they weren't back and beyond angry I had no way of contacting Lucifer. No matter how hard I'd tried. I swore to Christ, when Lucifer got his ass into gear and showed up, since apparently a couple of weeks didn't mean two weeks in his books, if he appeared without knowing my men were in his world, I would carve him open and feast upon his insides with pleasure. He had to know something.

"Right, that's fucking it," Nate clipped as I started brushing the wall with more paint. I ignored his words. He'd been threatening to beat my head against the wall for the last week. I knew he was all talk. "Vampire, are you ready?"

"I've been ready for some time, wolf," Asher answered, his voice low and thick. Slowly, I turned, and the paintbrush dropped from my hand. Both of my men were getting undressed.

"W-What's going on?"

They didn't say anything, just removed their pants like they already had with their tops and shoes. Nate's body shimmered and shifted; his half form shot forward. His tail swished back and forth. I wanted to rush over to him and play with it. My clit pulsed and my nipples hardened. Nate drew in the scent around him, and he shot me a cocky smile.

"Already turned on, angel?"

I gave him the finger. He chuckled around his sharp teeth. My gaze went to Asher as he hissed. His body had grown a little. His claws lengthened, his eyes glowed, his fangs dropped, and he licked his lips, watching Nate like he was a delicious meal. Asher's long, dark hair blew from the open window behind him. Usually he kept it tied back in a braid, but tonight this wasn't the case, and it made him look like an incredibly hot monster.

Both had my body shaking with need.

In a blink, Asher was beside Nate, picking him up and throwing him into the wall. The room shook. I expected some guards to rush in, but the door stayed closed. Nate jumped to his feet and rushed at Asher. He leaped, wrapped his arms around Asher's neck, and swung his body over Asher's back with his arms still locked around his neck. I expected Asher to be flung over Nate's shoulder, but Asher flipped himself over and wrapped his arms around Nate's waist. I would have been worried for both of them, if it wasn't for the erections they both sported—turned on from the fighting.

Nate bucked, but Asher didn't move; in fact, as Nate growled, Asher hissed into his neck before latching his teeth onto Nate's shoulder. Nate let out a roar before stilling for a moment, and the roar turned into a rumble of his chest. Asher's hand glided down and wrapped around Nate's hard-on, stroking him up and down.

My knees wobbled. I sank to the floor on my knees and kept my gaze on the two beautiful monsters.

Asher licked at Nate's neck before saying, "Do you hear, wolf, our mate—well, she's not yours yet, but listen to her heart pattering in her chest. Smell her desire. She likes a show, but are you ready for *me* to claim *you*?"

"Never," Nate clipped. He unleashed his claws, dropped his hands, and stabbed them into Asher's thighs. Asher snarled. His eyes swirled from green to black, something I hadn't seen before, and back again. If I had to guess, I would say it happened because his vampire was pissed.

I knew I'd been right when Asher's hold dropped from Nate for a second, only to come back and rake his nails up Nate's stomach and chest, leaving blood-welling red marks. I nearly missed Nate shuddering against Asher. Then he picked Nate up and threw him across the room. Before Nate could even get up, Asher flashed to his side. A low growl was Nate's only warning before Nate was picked up and thrown against another wall. Only Nate landed on his feet in a crouch this time and stood as Asher reached for him again. Nate's arms went around Asher's waist, and he slammed them to the floor. His hands snapped out to hold Asher to the floorboards. They snarled, hissed, nipped, and growled at each other.

"Open your legs, vampire. Let me have you." Nate's voice was rough and deep. His tail… well, it wagged in excitement while he ground their cocks together, causing Asher to still for a second, but when Nate's feet slipped between Asher's and started to spread Asher's legs apart, the vampire smiled up at him. Only, it wasn't a pleasant one.

I gasped when their bodies floated up to a standing posi-tion. Asher leaned closer to Nate, their arms still held together above their bodies. "Not happening, wolf. *I* claim *you*."

Nate snapped his teeth in Asher's face. Asher laughed darkly. He managed to free one hand and dropped it around

Nate, where his cute, fluffy tail swayed side to side. Somehow, I'd spread my legs without thinking about it and was rubbing my fingers over my jean-clad pussy as I watched Asher circle his hand around the base of Nate's tail. It stopped moving.

Nate's warning growl echoed around the room, and then it was Asher's turn to fly into a wall. Before he did so, Asher spun in the air and landed on his feet. He pushed the hair out of his face and grinned.

I blinked when Asher disappeared from sight. Nate's growl grew louder as he spun this way and that.

"Wipe that smile off your face, angel," Nate snarled at me.

I didn't realize I'd been smiling, but I couldn't wipe it away if I tried. I liked what I could see. I also enjoyed Nate calling me angel a lot.

A breeze swept over me. A whisper touched my ear. "Take your clothes off, love." Another breeze and Asher was gone. I heard a slap, and Nate cursed, snarling at the air as he rubbed his butt cheek.

Covering my mouth, I laughed silently but stood and quickly undressed. Nate's nostrils flared, and his dark gaze swung to me. His growl turned rougher. His eyes stayed locked on me as I made my way to Alex's bed.

Asher winked at me from where he leaned against the wall behind Nate. My vampire was playing a game of distraction to get what he wanted, and it was working because Nate never wavered from looking at me.

This was fun.

A thrill shot to my pussy, wetting me more than I already was. Nate breathed it in and took a step forward. He shook his head and glanced around the room. Asher was already on the move, flashing so unbelievably fast that we couldn't keep an eye on him. Nate snarled, reaching out, trying to grasp the invisible.

Feeling playful myself, I also wanted to gain the one bond I hadn't. Nate would be mine... and in turn, if Asher claimed Nate, then it wasn't my fault. Not when both of them turned me into a lusty mess.

I climbed onto the bed. Nate, hearing the squeaks of the mattress, whipped his eyes my way. Smiling, I lay on my back. He was close to the end of the bed, so when I dragged my legs up to place my feet on the bed and then spread them, he had a straight line to my drenched pussy.

He sucked in a harsh breath and took a step my way, only to stop, shake his head violently, and then glance around the room, searching for his prey.

I needed to play dirty to get his attention focused only on me.

I lifted up on one elbow and slowly glided my hand over my breasts and moaned. His dark gaze shot right back to me, and he let out a louder rumble.

"I know what you're doing, angel. It won't work."

I shook my head. "I don't know what you're talking about."

His upper lip raised, and he snarled, knowing I was lying. Yet, he didn't take his eyes off me. Instead, his gaze drank me in. It roamed over my skin, heating my body more. I moved my hand down over my belly, where it quivered under my own light touch. I then dipped my fingers into my curls and watched Nate take another step toward me, his hands fisting at his sides. His erection leaked at the tip, and I wanted to lick it away.

At the first touch with just one finger to my sensitive and throbbing clit, I threw my head back and moaned again.

Next, my hand was thrown away from my pussy, and there was a beast of a man between my legs, taking in his first taste of me. His tongue swiped over my folds, then from the bottom of my slit to the top where he circled his tongue around my nub. I cried out, lying flat on my back and gripping the sheets.

"Oh God," I yelled, and felt Nate's lips and mouth stiffen on me. A warm sensation started in my chest and weaved low to where Nate was connected to me. Nate stilled for a moment, then growled, which vibrated over me, causing me to twitch. It was then I remembered Thorn's words. Any sexual fluids would complete the bond; it just happened to be while Nate was between my legs. His hands and claws dug into my thighs, holding me tighter while the bond heated to the painful flame and then disappeared. Nate groaned. A burst of crazed desire shot into me. Desire, respect, annoyance, and even love... I knew it was all from Nate because I felt the same for him and made sure he could feel my own emotions.

He groaned again before giving me one last swipe of his tongue and climbed up to hover over me.

"The bond's complete," he stated.

Smiling, I nodded and cupped his cheeks. "Yes." I ran a finger over his plump, wet bottom lip. "Now kiss me, my mate."

He nipped at my finger. "You're annoying."

"So are you."

"You're a pain in my ass."

I laughed, feeling so much lighter. "So are you."

"I... care about you."

My heart thumped hard. "I know." I lifted up and pressed my mouth to his. Against his lips, I whispered, "And I care about you."

He grunted. "Good." His arms wrapped around me. He

captured my mouth in a demanding, hot, hard kiss while he slid his hard cock inside me. He ate my whimper into his own mouth, and if he didn't feel so good, I would have smacked that cocky smirk off his face.

Only his mouth then lifted off me, his head turned, and a snarl ripped out of him. Looking over his shoulder, I saw Asher with his hand wrapped around Nate's tail, stroking it up and down.

Nate had been claimed.

A giggle escaped me. Nate gave me a dirty look, but then pulled out from within me and thrust in deep. "Yes," I cried and saw him smile, until his growl came back, and he glanced over his shoulder again.

I couldn't see where Asher's other hand was. When I saw Nate's eyes widen, he pumped himself in and out of me and bit on his bottom lip, all while his chest rumbled with the same growl.

"Yes, wolf, fuck our mate," Asher bit out.

Nate did. His hips moved faster, but then he stilled. His growl changed up a bit, one of warning.

"I told you, wolf. You're mine," Asher said, and then I felt a powerful thrust. Nate threw his head back and roared. Asher's hand dug into Nate's hips, and then we were all moving together. I clamped my legs up around both men to feel Asher move in and out of Nate while Nate entered me again and again.

Nate's head dipped. His mouth latched on my nipple and sucked. It drew the orgasm straight up and out of me. My walls clamped around Nate's cock, and he groaned. Asher hissed behind him, their hips still moving back and forth, and then Asher bit into Nate's shoulder and both of them shuddered above me, moaning.

Nate panted into my neck. "We're doing that again, but it'll last longer, and I'll have you, vampire."

Asher chuckled. I could already see both of my men were back to their other selves. "I'd like to see you try again, wolf."

I loved their teasing, their friendship, and even their love for each other. They may not admit it to one another, but I could feel it from both of them, and it wasn't just aimed at me.

CHAPTER FOURTEEN
PAIGE

My body had recharged with a good round of lovemaking, a shower, food, and sleep. I'd never get over the separation anxiety I felt for Alex and Thorn, but I had to pull myself together and make sure I was still there for the mates I had around me. And for my people and my family too—a family who had banned me from their suite because they were sick of seeing me… sick of my moods, sick of my interfering in their own lives.

Okay, I probably went too far when I told Eric he needed to knock my sister up because she wanted another child. And that if he didn't do it, I was sure she'd find someone around the place who would easily take her to bed and impregnate her.

Yes, it wasn't my best moment. Especially since Yasmin had confided in me quietly how Eric said he didn't want any more children, but she did.

Thankfully, when I went there that morning, dropped to my knees and begged for forgiveness for being over-the-top stupid, Eric sighed, nodded, and let me in. Asher was off seeing to something, so I had Nate following me into their home close behind. In fact, since the bond completed, he hadn't left my side, and I lost count of the times he buried his nose in my neck to draw in my scent.

I didn't mind at all; in fact, I thought it cute.

Just after I'd entered my sister's quarters, I was attacked.

It had only been a couple of days, but when the kids wrapped their little arms around me for a hug, it felt like I'd been missing them for years.

Yasmin stood in the doorway to the kitchen with her arms crossed and a glare fixed on her face. I offered an apologetic smile. She turned and walked back into the kitchen.

"Is Mommy cranky with you?" Sophie asked in a whisper before she ran and jumped into Nate's arms. He spun her, causing her to giggle.

"She sure looks it," Oscar said.

I ruffled his hair and told him, "It's fine. I'll go talk to her." I glanced at Nate. "Wait here, please." He grunted and then was too busy defending himself when Oscar charged him and leaped onto his back. Nate fell, pretending with them. There hadn't been many moments I'd seen him with my niece and nephew, but when I did, I loved watching their interaction. Actually, I loved all of my men and how easily they melted around the kids.

I quickly pushed that thought aside, or it would lead me down a path I wasn't ready to travel. One that was probably filled with longing and hope.

When I entered the kitchen, Yasmin stood leaning against the counter. I smiled again, but she didn't return it.

"Sisters before misters. You always said that," she told me.

"I have." I nodded.

"What you told Eric was hard, cruel, and could have damaged our marriage."

"I know, and I'm so sorry. I've been crazy since Alex and Thorn haven't returned to me."

Her eyes softened a little. "I understand, but you're never to interfere in my marriage again."

"I won't. I promise."

"Okay," she said.

"Okay as in you'll forgive me or just okay?"

"I'll forgive you. Just this once."

I ran at her and hugged her tightly. "I am so very sorry."

She curled her arms around me. "I know you are. I also know you have a lot on your plate. The battle didn't go unnoticed, and then with the news of Alex and Thorn, plus with the visit from Lucifer, which I still can't believe, a lot is going on."

I nodded. "There's so much to deal with." I pulled back, my smile sad. "You know I was always the procrastinator on many things in life, but now it seems everything is just flying at me so fast it's hard to deal with. It's hard to get my head around, but I have to, and not only for myself but for the people depending on me."

She tucked my hair behind my ears and then rested her hands on my shoulders. "You're not alone in dealing with everything, Paige. You must remember you have your mates, you have us, the guards, the wolf pack now. You have so many who are willing to help you in any way. Even to help you get through your emotions. Just lean on us all a little more. It's okay to feel worry and fear for those you care about."

Nodding, I stepped back. Her hands dropped, and I started pacing. "Everything is still so new. I'm not sure how I'm supposed to act, what I'm supposed to tell people. I feel like a failure for showing my emotions. I need to show strength."

"The queen can show her people it's okay to care. It's okay to lose it when something bad happens. It makes you human... well, not human, but more approachable, more like the people who look up to you."

She was right. I tried to push my emotions down and do things that kept me busy to hide showing my emotions. I didn't need to hide them. Everyone felt, and even though I was the queen, I could still be me.

Stopping, I faced Yasmin. "You're right."

"Thank you, but another word of advice. What the queen shouldn't be doing is trying to fix plumbing, nearly burning down the kitchen, and decorating. Leave that up to the rest, the ones who know what they're doing."

A laugh escaped me. "I will."

"I'm glad. One last thing."

"Yes?" I said hesitantly.

"What the hell are you wearing?"

I glanced down at myself and laughed. "Alex's shirt and Thorn's pants."

"They are way too big for you. You look like a child."

I smiled. "I know, but they're comforting. There is something I could use your help with."

"What's that?"

"I have that ceremony this afternoon, can you help me pick the right dress for it?"

She snorted. "I think it's best I do."

"I love you, Yasmin."

"And I love you."

My sister was the best in the world.

"Will you fucking quit doing that?" I snapped, but not too harshly. I couldn't have made it harsh even if I wanted to because, even though I was pissed and concerned for Alex and Thorn, I was still happy, and that shit made me feel guilty because I didn't have my other mates here to share the happiness I got from Paige and Asher.

Christ, I was a ball full of fucked-upness.

"No, I don't believe I will, wolf," Asher said at my back as he nipped on my neck and continued purring. His vampire fucking purred. He was too damn satisfied after we'd fought again, and he'd managed to win. Though, I was sure my wolf was happy to give up if we got to feel the way he made us the night before. I hid my grin in the pillow. We knew we had to move, but we were being lazy. I was on my stomach with Asher practically covering my body with his weight. I liked it. Never thought I'd say that shit, but I did.

Paige walked out from the bathroom with a towel wrapped around her. She'd only left the bed moments ago after sucking me until I came down her throat while I enjoyed eating her pussy as Asher fucked me. "Are you both still agreeing with Yasmin with her choice of that?" She pointed down at the dress over the lounge chair. I didn't even look at the fabric. I couldn't stop looking at her gorgeous body, knowing she was mine.

Ours.

Christ, I was one lucky wolf.

"It's perfect, love," Asher said, running his claws up and down my back, drawing out goose bumps.

"For the millionth time, she picked well," I told her, then winked. She grinned, her eyes warm as she looked at us. Even the night before and moments ago, I never once sensed jealousy, and she'd kept our links open. In fact, I knew for certain she enjoyed a fucking lot watching Asher and me together. It'd be the same when I took Alex and Thorn as well.

All of us were made for each other. Shit. Being with a guy had never been in my thoughts until Paige came into our lives and blew our minds wide open. Though, I thought perhaps I was the only one who hadn't been with a guy previously. It was safe to say I'd been missing out.

Paige was our heart and soul. She was everything.

We had the perfect pack.

Even though my wolf and I hadn't claimed Asher in the way we had Alex and Thorn, we still saw him as ours, and the possessiveness was still the same over him that it was for them. Found that out only a couple of hours ago when a bitch of a vampire checked him out as we'd walked down the hall. I'd known where her thoughts had gone, and they were picturing him naked. It was lucky Asher was fast or she wouldn't have any eyes to look at him again.

Of course, the fucker thought it was funny, until someone brushed up against me in the kitchens, and Asher had her body flying through the room. It was lucky Paige had already changed things, and people seemed happier about said changes around the place because they found our actions cute. At least that was what Gregory told us on the walk back to Paige's room.

"Are you two getting ready any time soon?"

"Or you could come back to bed with us, angel," I said.

She pointed a finger at me and wiggled it side to side. "Don't tempt me, Nate. But, can I just say I love this… seeing you both like this. Happy." Her smile dimmed.

"Don't, love. Don't feel guilty for feeling happy in the moment because Alex and Thorn aren't with us. They will be eventually. They aren't lost to us forever. I'm sure of it. I'm also sure they'll want to hear about everything they've missed. Like the vampire beating the wolf."

I growled in the back of my throat, even though my wolf wasn't present since he was sleeping contently. "Be smug, vampire. It won't last."

Paige giggled. When I shot her a glare, she covered her mouth to try and hide it. I couldn't keep the glare when she was so fucking adorable. Also, when I felt fucking happy.

Goddamn, I wished Alex and Thorn were here.

"Come here, angel."

She shook her head. "I can't. You'll distract me, and we have to get to the ceremony soon."

I held out my hand while Asher went back to kissing and purring over me. "Come on, just for a little while."

Her lips thinned as she thought it over. Then she moved toward the bed and sat on the edge. I curled my arm around her waist and dragged her down, lifting enough to lay half over her. "This is better," I said.

She smiled. "I never would have thought that the big bad wolf was a cuddler."

"I never have been, but you're a bad influence on me."

She ran her hand through my hair. "I'm glad."

I hummed under my breath and rested my head against her shoulder. Asher's hand left my back, and I knew when Paige's hand disappeared from my hair that he'd taken it in his hand. I heard his kiss to her skin.

He leaned over me more so he could see Paige. "Back to what you were saying, love. I can only speak for myself, but I have never been this happy in my existence. What we have is beyond what I could have imagined in finding my perfect clan. You all complete me, and I look forward to the future we'll have."

I grunted. "Not long ago, I was thinking the same. Only I would have said pack, and I wouldn't have been that corny to say you complete me, but I'd think it."

Asher's fangs raked over my skin, his growl playful. "As soon as Alex and Thorn are home, we will tell them the same."

She licked her lips, which was distracting. "It hasn't been the same without them, and yet…."

"It has because we've all been together."

"Yes," she admitted guiltily.

"I know it's impossible not to feel guilty because I feel it as well, but we just have to remember that they're not lost to us. They will come back, and we'll all feel whole again," I told her. "It's not bad to be happy, to enjoy us, and for me to enjoy you both, and the same for Asher."

She nodded. "I know. I'll feel better when they are home."

"And they will be soon," a new voice drifted over us. Paige let out a scream. Asher's weight shifted as he flashed up and in front of us while I lay over Paige more, protecting her. Alma stood just inside the door. She rolled her eyes and waved her hand. "Oh, stop hissing at me, vampire. I come in peace."

"Maybe, crazy lady, come at a time when we're not fucking naked and in bed," I suggested angrily.

"How did you get in here?" Asher demanded.

She lifted a key in her hand.

"How did you get that?" I clipped.

Paige let out a muffled noise.

Fuck! I pulled back so I wasn't covering her face.

"Alma, what are you doing in here, and stop looking at my men like they're candy!" she demanded. "Asher, get some clothes on," she snapped.

Alma cackled, her hand covering her stomach while she kept laughing.

"Alma," Paige bit out. Annoyance swept through me, which came from Paige, and I knew she'd been feeling my rage. She ran her hands up and down my back.

"Right, yes, as I was saying, you all better get dressed."

"You didn't say that at all," I growled.

"Doesn't matter. Lucifer is on his way. I'm sure you'll want to greet him in the throne room."

Paige went to sit up, but the towel had slipped down and her breasts were on display. Even though the crazy woman was old enough to be her grandmother, she wasn't seeing Paige's tits.

"Thank you, Alma. We'll prepare," Asher said.

In other words, get the fuck out.

Alma snorted, obviously reading the brush-off. "Toodaloo." She waved and left.

"Wait," Paige yelled, but the old woman didn't return. Paige looked up at me. "What do you think she meant before?" Her eyes widened, and my heart stalled.

Both of us realized at the same time. While Asher chuckled at us, I bolted off the bed and ran to the bathroom, only to rush back and help Paige out of bed. I kissed her swiftly but hard and then said, "They're coming back." I reached out, sensed Asher close, and grabbed him, dragging him into our huddle.

She laughed cheerfully and shook us both. "They're coming home."

"They are, love. Let us prepare for them, and for Lucifer."

Shit. Forgot about that fucker.

CHAPTER FIFTEEN
PAIGE

Dressed in the long black gown my sister picked out, I paced the staged area of the throne room. In a rush, we sent word to my people that the ceremony would be delayed due to Alma foreseeing the arrival of Lucifer, finally. Of course, mentioning his name put people in a nervous tizzy. No doubt the castle would be spick-and-span in an hour or so.

I probably should have been scared knowing the devil was on his way, but nothing could override the glee I felt knowing Alma had seen that Alex and Thorn were coming home too. They must have got a hold of Lucifer in Hell somehow, and he was bringing them back to me.

I glanced at the doors again and saw Felnick shake his head. He was on the lookout for them. He also had guards lining the walls in case something bad happened.

Again, no fear bombarded me even thinking that.

It was probably stupid, but I trusted Alma would have warned us in some cryptic way if Lucifer was coming here to harm us.

"My queen, are you sure you won't wear the crown?" Gregory asked for the fifth time.

Rolling my eyes, I looked down at him where he stood below the steps of the stage. "No. No and no. I'm not a crown-wearing kind of woman."

"But… it will show Lucifer—"

"Nothing. I promise I'll wear it when it's necessary, like… I don't know, public meetings with royalty."

"Lucifer is royalty," he said, his voice high and anxious.

That was true. Damn.

I looked to the crown on a cushion in his hands. It gleamed with diamonds, rubies, sapphires, and other types of jewels. The thing was over the top and in the face.

"Fine," I grumbled.

Gregory beamed. He raced up the steps, but Nate moved to my side, grabbed the crown from the cushion, and set it on top of my head with a smirk. Unfortunately, it wasn't the time to junk punch him.

"Fucking hell, this shit is heavy." If I wasn't a ghoul, the weight of the crown could possibly break my neck.

"I've always found crown-wearing annoying myself," a new voice said into the room.

We froze for a second, and then Asher had Gregory out of sight before he flashed back to stand in front of me. Nate was at my side, his arm out, curling around my stomach, holding me back. Guards rushed toward us, but in a blink, they froze.

"No need for that."

I peeked around Asher to see a tall, dark-skinned man wearing a navy blue suit with a white shirt under it opened at the neck, dipping down his smooth mocha skin. It fit him to perfection. His piercing blue eyes crinkled at the corners, humor evident. His lips curved up in the corners. His black hair was shaved low, and for a second, I felt like I wanted to run my hand over it.

I shook my head. Grabbing Nate's arm, I moved it from my body. He was hesitant until I looked at him and smiled with a nod. He grumbled under his breath but dropped his arm. I stepped around Asher and moved in front of him instead.

"Lucifer, I presume." He was nothing like I'd imagined. Maybe what didn't help was how I'd watched the show *Lucifer* on Netflix.

"And you would be correct, my dear." His voice was made for sin. Smooth, rich, and something I could listen to all the time. Damn him.

"How did you get in here?" I asked, trying to seem unfazed. He stood there alone. I wanted to demand where my men were, where his people were, why had he shown without announcing himself? But I realized he would be all about games, and it would come down to how well I played them.

He chuckled. "I have my ways." His eyes went behind me to Asher, then slowly slid to Nate. I wanted to punch him in the face for staring at them too long.

When they moved further to the side, and I heard a whimper, I called, "Thank you, Gregory, that will be all." I heard a door slam, and then a grinning Lucifer was back looking at me. "Why wasn't he frozen? And if you wouldn't mind—" I swung my hand out toward my guards. "I promise they won't attack."

"So that man wasn't a mate?"

"Gregory?" I laughed. Lucifer nodded once. "No. My guards?"

The room erupted in the noise of my guards rushing forward. "Stop," I yelled. They did. "Please, go back to your positions."

Lucifer, with a smile, watched as my guards went back to the walls around us. He met my gaze and said, "You'll promise my people will be safe?"

"I promise, as long as none of your people harm mine in any way, yours will be safe."

He chuckled. "Very good, Paige. Perfect wording." His hand flung out and people appeared around him. Three women and six men—all dressed immaculately, except for a guy at Lucifer's side. He was dressed in jeans and some band T-shirt. His messy black hair held a tinge of blue to it. His eyes, which looked like a black abyss, held mine, and I couldn't seem to look away.

"Paige Alice, I would like you to meet…." I heard him sigh. "Is she listening to me?"

I licked my suddenly dry lips when the corner of rocker guy's lips lifted. He stood in a casual posture, his hands down at the sides of his slim waist. I just knew he would be perfect, like my men were, under his clothes, and I wanted to know what his caramel skin tasted like.

"My queen," Asher called.

Slowly, I drew my eyes from rocker guy and looked up at Asher. He dipped his chin down toward Lucifer.

Oh shit. Had he spoken?

I faced the devil again. He looked annoyed with his arms crossed over his chest. "Are you listening now?"

I nodded, but then a deep chuckle touched my ears. It came from Lucifer's side, and I slid my eyes to rocker guy. Our gazes caught and locked. He winked, and a thrill trembled throughout my body. My nipples hardened.

The rocker guy's body jerked forward. I realized Lucifer smacked him in the back of the head. My power burst forward, my heart beating louder, harder. My eyes glowed, my claws shot out, and through my long, sharp teeth, I snarled, "Don't." I glared down at the man I wanted to hurt for doing such a thing.

"Don't?" Lucifer whispered.

The room shook. More power threaded through the air, swaying clothing and hair around. Before my eyes, Lucifer changed. His eyes bled black. No white showed at all. He grew taller, larger. His shirt and jacket disappeared as wings sprouted from his back. His own claws held a silver-tipped edge. He didn't just have one set of teeth, but two, all long, pointy, and no doubt sharp.

"Did you tell me don't?" he demanded, his voice hard, cold, and vibrating around the room. Some of my guards shook from where they stood. His people watched on, either bored or with a smile. While Asher went all vampire and Nate half shifted, Lucifer's suit tore as his body expanded.

"Yes," I hissed. "I fucking told you don't. You don't harm anyone under *my* roof."

"*He* is one of mine. I can do to him what I wish."

I took a step forward. Both my men moved with me. Nate growled in the back of his throat, and Asher's own chest rumbled.

"Not here. This is *my* domain. You do not rule here. *I do*. I will do everything I can to protect people I see being hurt for no reason. Fucking touch him again and you'll see how that goes for you."

In the back of my mind, I knew this was crazy. I knew I should be cowering from the force of Lucifer's power licking and burning my skin, but I couldn't stop. I couldn't back down. I wasn't weak, and I would do anything to protect the guy beside him. Why? I didn't know, but the need to drag him to my side and curl around him, shielding him with my own body from any harm was strong. I was sure I would kill anyone who laid a finger on him.

This is stupid, Paige. He's the fucking devil. I tried to talk myself down. It could have worked if Lucifer hadn't started reaching for the man beside him because then all I saw was red.

I ran and sprang at Lucifer, ready to take him to the ground and rip his head off while I plunged my hand into his chest and dragged out his heart.

But I froze.

In midair.

My body was literally frozen in midair.

I could still hear, still see and move my eyes, but my body wouldn't move. By the sound of Asher's hisses and Nate's snarls, both of them were in the same predicament. I glanced at the guards and saw them frozen.

I'd fucked up big-time.

We were screwed.

Lucifer was going to rip us all apart and feast on our own bodies. He'd hunt my people down and kill them... all because of me.

Even when I thought I was doing the right thing, when my instincts were running my mind and body—and were usually right—I'd been wrong.

I wanted to cry, to scream and beg for my men, for my people. I wanted to ask to spare everyone and take my life only.

Before me, as Lucifer stepped close, his body morphed back into his human guise. Only his wings didn't disappear; he used them to float up to get in my face.

He studied me, then flew around to face his people. "She is ferociously beautiful, is she not?" No one commented. He spun back to me. "I think I might take this time, while you're not going for my throat, to introduce you to my people. Do you agree?" He cupped his hand behind his ear. "Oh, wait, that's right; you can't speak right now. Not to worry, my dear, I'll go on." His feet landed back on the ground, and he stood before the woman. "These are my concubines. Corazon, Aretha, and Virginia." For the first time, I actually took them in. Corazon looked like a young version of Salma Hayek, Aretha looked a twin to Halle Berry, and Virginia, well, she looked like Charlize Theron. Of course he would have women in his bed who were stunning. Virginia was the only one who smiled and waved at me. Lucifer kissed her neck while his other two glared at Charlize. He moved over to the men. "At the back, we have my loyal guards. Ozuna, Rami, Xi, Jair, and Glenn." I would have laughed at Glenn's normal name, if I wasn't damn frozen. For now, it was a good thing I couldn't move because I was sure I'd have kept laughing since his guards resembled Dwayne Johnson, Vin Diesel, Jason Statham, Bruce Willis, and Glenn looked like Chris Hemsworth when he starred in *Avengers*. I didn't know if they truly looked like that or if that was the form they'd picked. "Lastly, my son, Azrael."

As soon as I looked to his son, I was captured and lost in his dark, yet kind, gaze.

"For fuck's sake," Lucifer cried. I forced my eyes back to him. "So, you see, queenie, I can do what I wish to my own son since he's of my flesh and blood." He walked close to Azrael, who stood still and just stared up at me with a small smile on his face, while I wanted to yell at him to run.

Lucifer stopped behind his son. His hands rested on his shoulders in what seemed like a nice way, but I didn't trust it. I tried to yell, scream, and curse, but I couldn't.

"Do you like what you see here, queenie?" Lucifer asked, cupping his hand under Azrael's chin. Lucifer smiled. "I think you do. You're very distracted by him."

I tried again to move my mouth, my hands, my legs, but nothing.

"What about if I do this?" One claw popped out and he scraped it down Azrael's cheek. Blood welled and dripped down to his shoulder, his T-shirt.

My chest burned from my attempts to break free.

"No? You don't mind?" He laughed. "Then I guess I'll do this." He sliced across Azrael's neck, not cutting, but scratching, only I really didn't like to see it. To witness Azrael flinch. A savage howl started in my belly, swept up my chest and out my mouth. Only it was muffled.

Lucifer clapped and laughed. "Oh, she didn't like that at all." He grinned. "Hmm, let's see what else I can do to my own son." Lucifer walked around Azrael's body. All of his claws were out now, and he used them to slice at his son's shoulder, his arm, his chest, cutting through the material easily.

An untamed part of me ignited in my stomach. It went up in a blaze and burned bright throughout me. In the next second, my snarl was loud, free, just like my body, and I finished the jump to the ground, landing in a crouch.

Asher and Nate made noises behind me, but I couldn't look at them. I kept my eyes on the devil. My power still rolled over me. I pulled my upper lip up and snarled at him again. He was too close to what was mine.

Mine? I blinked at the word, confused.

Lucifer's hand reached out toward Azrael. Not wanting him harmed any more, I leaped. Arms stretched out, feet kicking off the floor, I grabbed Lucifer by the neck, hand circling, my own claws dug into his skin. We fell. Lucifer landed with a thud with me on top of him.

"Stop," he yelled. I didn't, but then I saw his hand out and knew he was talking to his guards. Then his hands were at my waist and he pushed, and I flew over his head, dropping to my back. I rolled, jumped up, and faced him again. He was already on his feet, spreading his legs, bracing. I moved in and jabbed my fist at his face. He dodged. I kicked at his legs, but he jumped them. His hand pushed at my chest, and I went crashing back into the pews. I got to my feet and charged, fist ready for his face, but I faked and then ducked, circling my arms around his waist. I took him to the ground, straddling his waist. I punched my claws into his chest. He cried out and grabbed my wrists.

Clapping started.

It had me pausing before I could reach his heart. I glanced up and saw Lucifer standing near his guards, still clapping. I looked back down and found nothing under me.

Lucifer beamed at me. "I do believe you are perfect."

CHAPTER SIXTEEN
PAIGE

Blinking, I stood and drew my power in as I backed up a little to stand in front of Azrael. "What is this?" I demanded at Lucifer.

"A test." Lucifer smirked.

I jerked my head back, confused. "A test?" When Lucifer stepped forward, I took one back, nearly tripping on my stupid dress. At least it hadn't been a hinderance when I fought.

I felt Azrael's heat. I wanted to face him, soak in it while I kissed and tasted him.

Why him?

What made him bring out my possessiveness like my men....

No, he couldn't be.

No. I had my men. I didn't need another one.

But why did I feel a connection toward him?

"Yes, a test, and you passed with flying colors, Paige Alice." Lucifer winked.

"A test for what?" I demanded.

"Not many can break my power, but you did. I'm impressed." He nodded with a big smile.

"That doesn't answer my questions, and can you please allow my men and guards to move?"

He shook his head. "Not just yet. I do believe they'll need to calm down first." He moved forward again.

I clenched my jaw, and Lucifer smirked. "Now, now, queenie. Don't get your panties in a twist. They'll be free as soon as I sense they have their rage under control."

There wasn't anything I could do, so I nodded. "While we wait, will you tell me what the—" A moan escaped me when a warm hand touched the back of my neck under my long hair. Spinning, the hand followed around to the front of my neck. I looked up into Azrael's dark eyes, startled by how familiar they seemed, and yet I couldn't place from where or why.

Azrael graced me with a smile, and I then realized his skin looked scratch-free. I reached out and touched his smooth cheeks, neck, and then he let me lift his T-shirt so I could make sure he'd healed... or had it all been a trick to begin with?

His hand covered mine over his chest. I glanced up. "No marks," I said.

He shook his head and lifted my hand back up to his cheek, flattening it there. His eyes closed, and he leaned into my touch as my heart hammered in my chest. I would have given anything to have kissed him right then. In fact, I started to lift up on my toes, since he was another tall man in my life, to take his mouth with mine. His eyes opened before he chuckled and shook his head. Humor danced in his eyes, along with desire. I hadn't read him wrong. He liked me, but why was he denying me a taste?

"This is sickly cute," Lucifer said dryly. I'd forgotten where I was and who was in there. I twisted back and moved into Azrael. My hands went behind me, to the thighs. Ready to protect him if I had to. Even when he chuckled at my back, his warm breath blowing into my hair. I wanted to smack him for laughing, but Lucifer spoke again. "But it can wait. We have other matters to speak of."

"What matters?" I asked.

"We shall adjourn to somewhere more comfortable with refreshments before we get started," he told me, and I didn't like being told what to do under my own roof.

Learn what fight to fight, Paige.

Sighing, I nodded, then thought of something. "We will, but first my men, guards, and then you'll need to tell me where Alex and Thorn are."

He eyed me impassively, which didn't last because then he laughed. "Demanding little thing." He looked to his son behind me and raised a brow. I didn't see what Azrael did, but it made Lucifer laugh again. "Fair enough, I would too."

He swept his hand out. My guards knew to stop as soon as they were free, so I wasn't worried about them. Nate's roar rolled over the room, as did Asher's snarl. The wind blew and Asher's vampire form stood in front of me. Nate shifted fully on his jump. He skidded and stopped in front of Asher, both wouldn't, or couldn't, stop the rumble from the chest in displeasure.

"Fine men you have, queenie, but it's unnecessary," Lucifer said.

I leaned around Asher to address him when two figures appeared between our group and theirs. My heart lurched, my body shook, and my belly swirled in delight. I shoved Asher out of the way. Somehow, I knew he let me move him or it would have been impossible, and then I dove at Thorn and Alex. Our arms wrapped around each other and a sob caught in my throat. Tilting my face up, I caught Thorn's lips first in an emotion-filled, hard kiss, then moved to Alex's mouth to do the same. My body settled and my heart soothed. I had my men back and in my arms.

"We're okay, sweetheart," Thorn mumbled against my neck.

"We're here now, dove," Alex murmured against my lips.

I pulled back enough to hit them both in the stomachs. They grunted. I heard laughter, but I grabbed them both close to me again and cried into their shoulders, overwhelmed with happiness at having them with me again. Their hands rubbed up and down my back while they soothed me with reassuring words.

"I love you both so much," I told them.

"Love you, Paige," Alex whispered into my hair.

Both their grips on me tightened. "I'll always love you, sweetheart," Thorn said softly.

"Neither of you will leave me again," I demanded.

Alex smiled and Thorn said, "We can only hope we won't ever need to." I knew they couldn't promise it, yet I wanted them to because it scared me to think it would happen again.

Sniffling, I buried my head back into them. I didn't want to let them go. I could have stayed there, in their arms, forever.

They were back.

They were with me. Home.

Elation had my head spinning.

My men were in my arms.

More warmth hit my back—Asher and Nate. They curled around us, and I felt whole again.

Whole, yet… rocker guy.

He should have been a part of this—a part of our family, our pack.

But I couldn't touch on that, not just yet, not when I'd just got Thorn and Alex back. If it wasn't for having to deal with Lucifer, I would have taken my men to the bedroom. Asher, Nate, and I would show them how much they'd been missed.

However, even with Lucifer and his people there, I lifted my head. Alex was the first to capture my mouth with his again. I moaned around his insistent tongue making his way into my mouth, knowing he needed this as much as I did. He finished with a quick peck, and I turned to Thorn. He was ready, his mouth on mine in seconds. His hand on my waist tightened its hold as we deepened the kiss. Both of us taking each other's whimper into our mouths.

Regrettably, I pulled back, then leaned back in to kiss his chest. I smiled a little shakily up at them. "It's good to have you both home."

"It's good to be home," Thorn replied.

"We're sorry for the fear you must have felt," Alex added.

I took a hand of each of theirs into mine and nodded. "I know."

"We took care of her," Nate said at my back. He thrust into my lower back. He thrust his *hardness* into me. My eyes widened, and I spun around.

"Nate, what have I said about being naked in front of people?" Rough laughter started, but I ignored it.

Nate grinned. "Alex?"

A click of fingers and then Nate was dressed in jeans and a T-shirt. I caught Alex brush Nate's hand as he stepped closer. "We knew you would both take care of her," he said.

Nate grunted. Then Thorn was there curving an arm around Nate's shoulders. I didn't miss the pressure he applied to Nate's arms. "We had trust in you both."

"As did we," Asher stated. "Though, someone had her moments." He smirked.

As I turned to Asher, ready to rant, his hand covered my mouth and he faced me back to Lucifer. Shit. Right. "Thank you, Lucifer, for bringing my bonded back to me."

"It was lucky my son found them," Lucifer commented with a grin.

My eyes shot to Azrael. He dipped his chin down, smiling.

"Thank you," I said again to the right man.

Thorn made a noise in the back of his throat. "Had no one—"

"We must adjourn," Lucifer called loudly. "We could use some refreshments and comfortable seats."

I drew my brows down. It certainly seemed like the devil was keeping Thorn from saying something, but what? I kept my gaze on Thorn. He shook his head, giving me a thin-lipped smile.

"My queen," Gregory said, appearing from somewhere. "I have set up the library for the meeting. It is most private for such types of things." Meaning he would have gotten anyone in that area, since it was close to Thorn's room, away for their own safety. This man was amazing.

"Thank you, Gregory." I faced Lucifer. "Shall we?"

"I believe so, my dear."

* * *

Lucifer sat across from me with his three concubines on the long leather couch while I sat leaning into the corner of a chaise lounge. Thorn stood on my right and Asher sat on my left. Nate had shifted back to his wolf form to sit on the floor at my feet, and Alex stood behind me with a hand on my shoulder. I was glad he did as I needed the comfort that he was back. Thorn may have sensed it as well because he reached down, resting his fingers lightly on my other shoulder.

Lucifer's guards, all but one, stood behind him. It was Glenn who was with Gregory helping with refreshments. Azrael stood over near the windows smiling. He seemed to always smile, and I wondered why. What made him so happy?

No one said anything as Gregory and Glenn puttered around. A wet nose touched my hand. I looked from Azrael to Nate, who jerked his chin toward Lucifer.

Fuck.

Had I been so lost staring at Azrael that I hadn't even noticed Lucifer's attention boring into me? Was he waiting for me to speak?

"Have some restraint, queenie," Lucifer said, his lips twitching.

I could feel my cheeks heating. He was right. I should have some since my own bonded mates were in the room and they were witnessing me lust over a demon—if he was even that. I didn't know. A man who was Satan's son. How could I have been so thoughtless? Did it show Alex and Thorn I didn't care they were back?

Nate snapped his teeth at Lucifer, sensing my turmoil.

Alex's hand pressed down. "My queen—"

I shook my head and then tilted it back to have his eyes. "Not my queen, never my queen from any of you. You're my bonded mates. We're one. A family." I reached out for Nate. "A pack and clan." I took Asher's hand. "I'll hurt anyone who tries to say it's disrespectful you call me by my name and not queen around them."

Alex's eyes softened, and he nodded. I glanced at Thorn, who smirked. "As you wish, sweetheart."

A female groaned. "How many more gag moments will we have to endure?"

I snapped my head to Aretha who'd spoken.

Leaning forward, I rested my elbows on my knees. "Whose house is this?" I didn't let her answer and went on in a darker tone. "Whose mates have just been brought back to her after two weeks of fear that I'd lost them forever? I will do what I want, whenever I want, and you can keep your mouth shut."

She spluttered, "You can't talk to me like this."

"Under my roof, I can. If I were in your domain, I would bite my tongue and think you were nothing but a bitch." I glanced at Lucifer, raising my brow to see if he was going to fight me on my decision.

"She's right, Aretha. This is her domain. She is alpha here. You're stupid to think you could act like that and your outburst didn't embarrass me." He glanced over his shoulder to Xi. "Take her back. Keep her locked in her room until I can deal with her."

"No, Lucifer, darling, please. I'll keep my mouth shut."

"No," he clipped.

Maybe I should have felt bad for getting her into trouble with the devil, but I didn't. She screamed as Xi approached, and when she sneered at me, I could see in her eyes what she'd planned before she even acted it out. She launched at me, her hands out ready to wrap around my neck. I wasn't sure why she thought she could attack me with all my men surrounding me, but she tried.

Yet, it wasn't one of my men who stopped her. Azrael, with speed that matched Asher's, flashed forward. His arm wound around her waist in midair, she jerked to a stop and then was thrown backward into the windows. They shattered, and she flew out them. No one seemed too bothered about it. Honestly, I wasn't sure how my own eyes could have followed the fast actions of Azrael, but they had…. Maybe it was another power of being queen manifesting.

"Xi," Lucifer ordered.

Xi disappeared from where he'd stood, but in the next blink, he was back with Aretha, struggling like a wild woman in his arms. But Xi stood holding her through her struggles, emotionless.

"Master?" he asked.

"Just take her back."

They disappeared.

"It is common for her to have outbursts at home. I didn't think she'd be foolish enough to do it here."

I nodded. I wasn't sure if I should apologize for speaking to her the way I did. After all, she was a concubine for Satan, but something held me back from saying anything. As I'd stated, this was my domain. I'd accepted the position. Claimed it. I would do what I wanted, when I wanted without comment from another. I'd never liked to be questioned even when I was a human, but now even more so.

With the tilt to Lucifer's lips, I knew I'd made the right choice by biting my tongue and not saying anything.

"Would you mind if we moved onto the matter of why you requested a meeting?"

"This is lovely," Virginia commented after a sip of tea.

I glanced from Lucifer to her. "Thank you."

I went to move my gaze back to Lucifer, but a grinning Virginia added, "You have a wonderful home."

Even though she seemed sweet, nicer than Aretha and Corazon, my attention was caught in a suspicious way. Why was Lucifer allowing her to interrupt as such? "Thank you again. I haven't been here long or even seen the village yet, but I do believe you're correct. It's beautiful."

"You haven't been here long and yet… I feel you've changed so much." She winked. "Impressive." She snuggled into Lucifer. "Don't you think, Luca?"

"I do, my lovely."

Virginia rested her head against Lucifer's shoulder as if they were on a date and watching a movie together. Something was going on. Something was about to happen, and I wasn't sure if it would be good or bad. Yet, I readied for it, and sensed my men around me do the same.

Her gaze moved to Thorn. "How well do you know a woman named Alma?"

I leaned forward. "What of Alma?" I demanded.

Virginia beamed up at Lucifer. "She's protective, isn't she?"

He chuckled. "That she is."

"What about Alma? She'll not go with you. She'll not work for you. She belongs here. We're her family."

To my utter shock, Virginia's eyes welled. "I have never met anyone walk into a leadership role and shine in their new position such as you have. Your love and kindness are beyond what I'd have imagined. It would be an honor to be claimed, as you would say, into your family." The air shimmered around her, and then I was looking at Alma cuddled up to Lucifer. "Thank you, dear."

CHAPTER SEVENTEEN
ASHER

Paige flung herself back into the couch. She wasn't the only one shocked. When Alma's body shifted back to Virginia's young one, she smiled once again.

"What's the meaning of this?" Thorn demanded harshly. Nate stood on all fours and pressed himself against Paige's legs. Alex's eyes change to purple. His magic swept out, and I could see the clear wall erected in front of us, keeping Lucifer and his people on the other side.

"Relax." Virginia grinned. "Paige is safe with us. She always will be."

"Who are you?" I clipped.

Lucifer's hard eyes locked onto mine, even my vampire side wanted to look away. Somehow, I managed not to, and I was sure it had to do with the woman in my life. Her power mixed with Alex's and Nate's when I'd fed on them, strengthening mine. My clan offered me more than respect and love. It gave me more power. It rolled through me and locked my body and then my eyes on the biggest threat in the room.

"Now, now, boys. We all know you're both tough. Cut it out." Virginia laughed. We both looked at her at the same time, so no one lost in the stare down, and I was happy with that.

"Again, could you inform us who exactly you are because right now it seems we have all been tricked into thinking you were the seer who had been with the former queen for a very long time. We find it unjust to have been lied to this whole time."

Lucifer nodded once at me, at my choice of words since they just bordered on respectful.

Virginia straightened, yet she still leaned into Lucifer. "Of course, I can understand why you're all confused." She took a breath. "The night before sweet Marsala gave her heart to our young Paige here, she requested an audience with my Luca. Since we'd been out on a date discussing a certain something, I went along with him. She'd asked us for a favor. After some thought, we complied, but of course, we had demands of our own. One was for me to come and stay in my twin sister Alma's stead to make sure.... It doesn't matter just yet. It is me who you met, not Alma, who is away on a holiday with her beau."

"Is it because of Alma being your sister why you've kept the secret of this community's existence?" I asked.

"Correct." Virginia smiled. "At first it was for my sister's sake to keep the secret of Marsala and her community from others. Now there have been other reasons we'll get into shortly." She moved her gaze to Thorn. "Yes?"

"It's been you all along?" Thorn asked.

"It has." She nodded.

"But how have you been seeing things?"

"Alma and I have the same power."

"And you've been helping us, why?" Paige asked.

Virginia shrugged. "I liked it here. I loved the people, but I saw Marsala had lost her authority among her people. The people who couldn't help themselves needed someone who would do it for them. As soon as I saw Paige arrive, and by the way she took control, I knew things were going to be amazing."

Paige waved her hand in front of her. "Wait, let me get this straight. Was it you or Alma who 'saw' it should be me to take Marsala's spot as queen?"

"Oh, that was Alma. It was me who knew Aggie would be a darling to have on board. Alma told me all about her, and as soon as I met Aggie myself, I loved her like a daughter I didn't have."

"You have two daughters, lovely," Lucifer added in.

"Bah, they're bitches. Aggie's not. It was also me who knew Clyde could be trustworthy. It was me in that room with you for the first time and since."

"Why?" Alex asked. Nate woofed; he too wanted to know why Lucifer's concubine stayed within the walls taking on a persona of her twin sister.

"There is another question I have," I said. It may not be a good time to interrupt the knowledge of getting to know why all this happened, but this question had me suspicious of the woman.

"Yes?" Virginia asked.

"How is it Alma is so much older than you appear now, if you are twins?"

Paige clicked her fingers and pointed my way. She sent me a wink as if to say "Good one, Asher."

"That's simple. It's because I've been living in Hell."

"You don't age down there?"

"No." A sad smile crept onto her lips. "I offered Alma some time down there with me, but… well, she doesn't like my Luca very much, and she has always believed aging is the way of God."

"I know this is getting off topic again," Paige started, looking away from the man who stood near our couch. I could sense something going on between the two of them. It felt very similar to the connection I'd shared with Nate, Alex, and Thorn the first time around Paige. Did that mean he was meant to be her bonded mate as well? There was also something very familiar about him. He'd already proven himself when he protected Paige from Lucifer's concubine. I just wished I knew all there was about him right then so I could encourage the connection Paige had with him. If it meant more protection for our Paige, then I would welcome whomever in, as long as Paige agreed to it as well. I was sure I wouldn't be the only bonded male of Paige's who thought like that too.

I shook my thoughts away as Paige continued. "But how did you have a life with Lucifer and your twin believe in God's ways?" Yes, we could all presume God was real, or how else would Lucifer be sitting on the couch?

Virginia giggled. "Simple really. I fell in love and would do anything to keep that love. It doesn't mean I don't believe in God's law-abiding ways." Lucifer snarled low, and Virginia patted his thigh. "I do, to some extent, but Lucifer has my heart over everything. I'm sure you can understand that?"

Paige glanced at all of us, leaving Azrael for last, albeit briefly, before she looked back to Virginia and nodded.

"Good." Virginia returned her smile.

"I'm surprised you allowed your concubine to stay here, Lucifer," Thorn said. That was true. I'd heard he was possessive to a point he'd killed people for looking at his women.

He smirked. "I have found it is easier to let my lovely have what she wants over fighting her."

Corazon snorted, picking at her nails. "She gets everything she wants."

"Corazon," Lucifer warned.

The woman rolled her eyes but said nothing. I was guessing she didn't want to be sent back.

"Why…?" Paige started as a blush coated her cheeks.

"Why does he have concubines when he has me?" Virginia asked, smiling.

"Yes." Our mate nodded.

"Well, they're used for a power source. I can't always be used, or it would drain me."

"How are they used as a power source?" Thorn questioned.

Virginia glanced up at Lucifer. He nodded. "Lucifer is an angel, but what many don't know is he also has another side to him."

"Vampire," I said softly. I knew a part of him felt like kin, but I'd brushed it off, thinking our darker sides had originated from Hell.

Virginia looked up at me and nodded. I could feel Lucifer's gaze on me, but I ignored it. No wonder we'd had a struggle of dominance. It was our vampire sides working against each other. Usually, I would have seen he was more dominant, but mine had become stronger since Paige and my clan had connected. Although, I wasn't stupid enough to believe I would win a fight with the devil. His abilities went beyond all of ours, which had me wondering yet again why they were here trying to get in Paige's good graces.

They wanted something from her, but what?

Did it also mean we'd have an alliance with Lucifer?

For Paige's sake and safety, it was something to take into consideration before making the final decision.

I ran my hand down Paige's thigh. She shivered. I left my palm flat just above her knee. Meeting Lucifer's eyes, I stated, "I would like to know the other reasons you are here. Why Virginia wanted to involve herself within these walls."

After a beat, he answered, "The demons who attacked Paige, to begin with, weren't sent from me. The first one, Valino, who encountered Paige, sensed her changes within. He sent a mental message to his brethren before he was killed."

The one in the restaurant. We hadn't thought he was strong enough to contact his brethren in Hell, unless they'd already been on earth of course.

"Does that mean they work alone?" Alex asked. "They were after Paige because they knew she would be queen and wanted to use her to gain their own kingdom?"

"There is always that possibility. I have many demons who are loyal to me, too fearful of what I would do. But there are always creatures in any domain that are trying to gain strength to overthrow me and anyone with power and authority." Those were things we'd already known, but then he added, "However, I fear the demons that are Valino's brethren are working alongside someone."

"Then they were the ones who ambushed us and were working with Grace," Alex said.

Paige's heart skipped a beat. Nate snarled and I tensed. None of us liked hearing his words. They were our clan, our family, and they were tricked. We could have lost them all together and it didn't sit well at all.

"Ambushed you?" Paige demanded in a low, vicious tone.

Alex pushed calm out to all of us. It was new. I could feel Alex, and not just through his link with Paige. It meant we were all connected on a new level. Nate's snarl dropped off into an unsettled growl in the back of his throat, and I relaxed a little, feeling his calm.

"Remember, dove, we're fine."

The sound of her teeth grinding together reached me. She nodded once.

"What happened?" she clipped.

They told us the story of what they'd been through, and in return, we filled them in on the battle with Grace.

"I wished we'd kept her alive so I could kill her again," Paige stated.

"I'd also like to get my hands on her," Thorn said, his jaw tight. "In fact, I could do with a snack."

Lucifer chuckled at that.

I interrupted with "Do you know who the demon working with Grace was?"

Lucifer nodded. "From what Alex described, he is Rebellious. He'd been a guard, but when I'd caught him," his jaw clenched, "flirting with Virginia, I handled him. I thought he was dead. Obviously, I was wrong. I have no doubt he would be working with the same people who are trying to capture Paige."

"Why are they after her?" Alex asked.

"With Paige comes power and her people. There's been a rumor that if a demon was to eat the ghoul queen's heart, her power and followers will be theirs."

"Is it true?" I demanded.

Lucifer shrugged. "No one knows because no demon has killed a ghoul queen."

"And no one ever will," I stated coldly and was surprised when Lucifer, the devil himself, nodded.

"How dangerous is Rebellious?" Thorn asked.

Lucifer shrugged. "Depends on who he works alongside.

On his own, any one of you could take him down. If he's able to gain more power, he could be a problem."

Fuck, we needed to know who he worked with. I had a feeling it was the council.

"Do you know of the council?" Alex asked.

Lucifer snorted. "Of course." His teeth ground together. "They're a group of people who think they're too powerful to be touched."

Virginia's hand landed on his. "My latest premonition involved the council, Luca."

His body locked. "What of them?"

"They've been informed of Paige's existence and whereabouts."

"And?" he clipped.

Virginia opened her mouth, made a gargle noise, and then frowned.

I spoke for her. "From what we gathered, if they are to come here for her, the chance of our survival is slim. If we pay them a visit, things look better." I paused for a moment and added something that had been on my mind. "However, I have been thinking, when we do go there, we will need people of the supernatural community to know of their... wrongdoings. We'll need proof to take them down without anything coming back on us."

Lucifer's lips tipped in the corners in a small smile. "I would agree with that assessment. Without proof and people seeing the evidence, things will go south for you all if you just show and murder the lot of them. You'll need others to see Paige and the good she's doing for her people, that aren't just her own kind."

Paige's hand shot out. "Wait. Hold on. Are you saying there's a chance, if we manage to take all of them down in the right way, nothing comes back to bite us in the butt? People will see me as their new… I don't know, council member?"

"Correct." He nodded.

Paige's panic hit us all. Quickly, I curled my arm around her and dragged her close.

"I won't do it." She shook her head. "Already I have enough on my plate here, and I struggle each day to make sure I'm doing it right."

"Already you're succeeding in ruling like all queens should be," Virginia said.

Lucifer nodded. "You rule like I do now. I respect it."

Paige gulped. We all heard it. I thinned my lips to keep from laughing. I didn't think she'd take that as a compliment having been compared to the devil.

Lucifer laughed. "I'll rephrase that, my dear. You rule like I do since Virginia came into my life. Before I had her, I killed anyone who pissed me off for the littlest thing. Now, she grounds me. We kill when necessary. We protect our people. We give orders when needed, and change things to match the times. Before Virginia, I didn't have respect from my people. They lived in fear. After her, they follow me for a different reason… because they want to."

"But… you're the devil," Paige said.

If it had offended, I was ready to flash her away, but it didn't. Instead, he smiled.

"I'll never be a saint. There were too many sins on my soul, and really it would be boring to live my existence as a good Samaritan like my dickhead brother Michael. But it doesn't mean I can't alter my world, or my thoughts for the people I love." He winked. "But back to what I was saying. If killing the council is the path you'll have to follow, you'll need to give the people something, or *someone* new."

"What about you?" Paige asked, hopeful.

Lucifer snorted, then chuckled. "No."

Virginia shook her head. "His life belongs in Hell. It's where he's needed."

Paige sagged against me. "My love, it's not something to worry about now," I told her.

"I agree," Thorn said. "Things aren't set in stone. We still need to find proof to take down the council, and this is before they even think about coming here."

"We should send a notice of our visit. So they know we're coming, and then they won't have to come here." Alex glanced at Virginia. "Would that work? Would they stay away and wait for us to come to them?"

Virginia winked.

"Gregory?" Paige called.

"I'll have it done by the end of the day, my queen."

"Thank you. Please state we'll be there within two months." She glanced to Virginia, who nodded, and then Paige smiled over at Gregory, who bowed. Paige's nerves were all over the place. She still feared a lot of things, but I could still feel her interest in Azrael, and also her arousal and happiness that she had her clan all together. What I also sensed was confusion.

"Sweetheart," Thorn called.

She tipped her head up to him. "Yes?"

"What has you confused?" He'd been reading her too, and no doubt, Alex and Nate had done the same.

She nodded, glanced back to Lucifer, and asked, "Why are you both helping us?"

When Virginia smiled up at Lucifer, he nodded. She looked back at Paige and said, "It's simple. We believe you're the best candidate to offer our support to for the future. All we're after is a peaceful existence." She paused a beat. "However, there is one more thing."

Paige's heart skipped a beat. "What's that?"

"We needed to make sure you would be the perfect mate for our son."

CHAPTER EIGHTEEN
PAIGE

"I'm sorry, what?" I mean, I knew there was a connection with Azrael, but I didn't realize Virginia was his mother. And my mate? I had four already. *Four*. What was strange was how I couldn't sense any unease from Thorn or Alex. They showed me nothing through the link, even though it was open. However, Asher was wary, and Nate pressed closer and growled low in concern.

"You. Are. Our. Son's. Mate," Lucifer said slowly and with sign language.

I wanted to punch him. Even more, I wanted to look at Azrael, but suddenly, I felt shy. Was this some type of arranged marriage? Were they for real? This was why they were supporting me, so they could get rid of their son? Were they mean parents? Of course they were mean, well, Satan was, because he'd cut his own son up… although there wasn't a mark on Azrael in the end.

"It's very amusing watching her as she thinks," Lucifer commented.

"True, so many emotions cross over her features. Right now, she's back to confusion."

"What was the screwed-up face one?" Lucifer asked.

"She was probably worried about everyone's sanity," Virginia answered.

Running a hand down my face, I suddenly stood and started pacing in front of my couch. Only that got me closer to

Azrael. My eyes widened. I looked away, so I didn't get lost in his eyes, and backed up, tripping over Asher's feet. Quickly, I jumped up, ignoring my face heating.

I pointed to a chuckling Lucifer. "You… he… this isn't…. I mean, you can't just offer up your son to me." I threw out my hand Azrael's way. "He looks like a nice guy, and he… ah, helped with your concubine trying to hurt me. Still… I have four bonded males already."

"Are you saying you don't feel the connection between you both?" Lucifer asked, now frowning.

I didn't want to admit it in front of my men. Yet, it was ridiculous to deny it since I attacked the devil himself trying to protect Azrael.

Biting my bottom lip, I nodded.

"So you do feel it?" Lucifer questioned again. I was sure it was to annoy me.

Glaring at him, I said, "Nodding does mean yes."

"Let me tell you a story then," he replied, ignoring my snark. In fact, he'd been very lenient with me. Was it because Azrael was their son and them thinking he was my mate?

I dipped my brows in confusion. "Story time now?"

"There's always time for story time. However, this is important right now." I nodded. He relaxed further into the couch while I took my seat back and didn't look at their son. "It started on a cold, dreary night—"

"Are you serious right now?" I demanded. His jaw clenched in reaction. "Is this an actual real story or something made up?"

"It's real. I'm just setting the mood."

I rolled my eyes. Who'd have thought the devil was a narrator? I thinned my lips and bit down on them when he started again with "It was a cold, dreary night in New York

City. I had been out looking for a certain someone when Marsala appeared out of nowhere."

I really wished he would just get to the damn point. But if I interrupted again, there was a chance he'd once more start from the beginning, and I couldn't have that happen.

"Marsala and I had known each other for a long time. I wouldn't say we were friends; however, she was a person I could rely on to deal with my wayward demons in her area. She needed a favor. A protector and teacher for her replacement."

I stilled.

Ezra? Sorrow grabbed at my chest. I quickly blocked my mates from my emotions. I erected a wall between us so I couldn't feel theirs either as I wanted to feel that pain. I deserved that pain.

"After some thought, I offered her someone since he was to be punished for disobeying us. You know who I'm talking about?" Lucifer asked.

I nodded. If I opened my mouth, I would have sobbed. Tears brimmed my eyes. Should I have cared it was in front of Lucifer? Probably. It showed weakness, but I'd already been gushy and loving in front of him, so I didn't care what he thought.

Then I wondered if they blamed me for Ezra's death. Had he been their faithful hellhound and I'd got him killed?

"He died under your care," Lucifer stated.

I nodded.

"You cared for him?"

I nodded.

"You still care for him?"

Another nod. I also wanted to shout at him to shut up, or I would burst into tears. Thorn took my hand, kissing the back of it. Asher's hand touched the base of my neck. Nate whimpered and rested his head on my knees. Alex's hand went to my shoulder, where he applied pressure.

All of them offering me their support.

I loved my men.

Loved them.

But whatever was to come, it was me who would deal with it.

"It was unfortunate to lose him. It—"

My lips unlocked, and I said darkly, "It wasn't unfortunate. It killed a part of me, and I'll forever feel his loss. He was my friend, my teacher, my companion, and if it wasn't for my men, my family, I would have found a way to end my life because it wouldn't have been worth living without him. I loved him. I still love him, and I always will. You can punish me for his loss because I would do the same since he was so special."

Sniffling, Virginia wiped at her eyes. "You really are perfect. The way you love is strong and with everything you have. Your body, heart, and soul. It's beautiful."

I ground my teeth together, not understanding what was going on.

"Azrael," Lucifer called.

Great, we were back to arguing over setting us up.

I opened my mouth to say something but snapped it closed. I really wasn't in the mood to speak, especially after talking of Ezra since thinking of him saddened me. All I wished for was to go to my room with my men and fall into bed with them, knowing they were all safe.

However, out of the corner of my eye, Azrael stepped closer. Asher stiffened, and Nate growled. I turned my head his way to tell Azrael we'd speak of it another day, if they were staying, when his body wavered, almost shimmering.

I snapped my lips closed. Heat washed through the room. It burned hotter for a moment, forcing me to close my eyes. Something was happening. Something to Azrael. Panic clutched my gut.

Then the heat stopped.

Asher muttered, "What the fuck?"

Nate whimpered. I glanced down to him to see him jump forward, then back. I shifted my gaze to where he was looking.

My jaw dropped. My eyes widened at where Azrael had been standing a moment ago. But….

It couldn't be.

I was seeing things.

I had to have been.

My throat closed, my eyes welled, and my heart pumped erratically in my chest.

Anger had me standing, had me shaking my head, fisting my hands at my sides. "How could you do this to me? It's not him. It's not. This is beyond cruel." Nate went to all fours and snarled.

Hands grabbed my shoulders. "Sweetheart," Thorn said, his voice thick with emotion. "Look at him. Really look at him."

I shook my head again and again. "No. I won't. Leave!" I yelled.

"Dove," Alex tried, coming to my side. His fingers glided through Nate's hair since he was just in front of me. "Just look. It is him."

"No," I sobbed.

Alex's free hand touched my jaw. He gently tilted my head his way to have my gaze. "Trust me?"

Sniffling, I nodded.

"Then look. Please." He threaded his fingers in mine and held on tightly.

I rubbed at my chest, trying to still my erratic heart. I was scared out of my mind it was a stupid, cruel prank. Slowly, I faced the hellhound that had been Azrael.

Azrael sat on his hind legs, letting me have my inspection. I ran my wet eyes over his silky, messy black fur and large stocky body. A spine full of jutting bones, razor-sharp teeth with two long fangs hanging out of his mouth. His jaw opened, his tongue rolled out, and he panted. I moved my gaze up to his red glowing eyes.

He looked exactly like Ezra, but it could still be a trick.

The hellhound stood and walked my way, moving as Ezra had. He stopped just in front of me, and through the red haze, I watched his eyes roll before his tongue came out and licked the side of my neck and cheek. His warm breath washed over me…. He even scented how Ezra had—of fire, earth, and honey.

Opening my eyes, I met its gaze. "Ezra?"

A rumble came from within his chest, and he dipped his head.

I made a noise in the back of my throat; a sob wanted to tear free, but I didn't allow it.

Thorn stepped up beside us. I glanced at him. He smirked softly. "He came to us in Hell. It was lucky he'd sensed Alex's power because we'd been stuck in a house full of demons. He saved us, took us back to his home, where he transformed into Azrael. We would have come home sooner, but we had to wait for Lucifer to return to his kingdom. Since Alex couldn't teleport out of Hell without his permission, Alex's power wouldn't work. Also, time in Hell moves a lot slower than here. It's only been a week for us."

Nodding, because all of it made sense and there wasn't anything they could have done differently, I reached out and ran a hand through his fur. He leaned into my touch. "How?"

It was Lucifer who spoke quietly. "When Marsala said she was in need of a guard for the new queen, it happened to be when Azrael was in trouble for disobeying us. We thought it would be good for his punishment."

"Also a learning curve," Virginia added. "He was spelled to stay in his hellhound form for added punishment. We didn't know you would form a connection. When he was… killed here on Earth, he was sent back to us in Hell. He told us what happened and since then has wanted to be back at your side."

Lucifer nodded. "However, he had to heal since he is part human, like his mother. The mage's power was able to work on him. If he was a full hellhound, it wouldn't have. Then, before I could get us here, I had things to attend to in Hell, which couldn't be put off."

Virginia giggled. "Our Azrael wasn't happy waiting. He tried everything he could to get back, but he doesn't have the power to open portals."

I bit my trembling bottom lip and drew my gaze back to Azrael. "I thought you were lost to me." Tears welled. Azrael whined and licked my neck and cheek again. My Ezra had never been one to think of personal space or what was gross.

"You wanted to come back to me?"

He nodded, his lips pulling back into a smile. Or a hellhound version of one.

Then a thought popped into my head. Everything that had

happened. Everything that I'd done around him. My eyes widened. "You watched me get dressed, and in the shower, and… " Heat hit my cheeks. Some nights he'd been in the room, and I'd touched myself, thinking he'd been asleep. Had he really?

He let out a huffing noise… the same sound Ezra made when I'd assumed he was laughing.

"Ezra—Azrael," I scolded.

His body shimmered and next in front of me stood the man.

"I prefer Ezra," he told me with a warm smile.

Fresh tears welled and fell. I wanted to reach out to him, to drag him into my arms and never let go. But this wasn't the Ezra I knew. This was a man I didn't know. How was I supposed to act? What was I supposed to do?

Everything in me told me to hold him, to— Why was that bitch looking at him?

Corazon's gaze slowly ran up and down Ezra. I wanted to punch her in the face so it dinted and she couldn't see out her eyes.

"Dove," I heard Alex say.

She licked her lips as if she remembered she'd had a taste of him. I ground my teeth together before lifting my upper lip at her. Only she didn't notice the threat. She didn't notice her life was dangling in front of her. She rubbed her thighs together, her gaze on Ezra's ass.

A growl erupted from my chest.

"Sweetheart," Thorn said, his hand touching my arm.

Laughter sounded in the room, but I ignored it, as did Corazon since she was lost in eye-fucking Ezra. She moved forward on the couch as if she would come at him.

"Grab her," Asher cried as I flew at the woman reaching

for Ezra. Arms curled my waist and drew me back into a hard body.

His scent calmed me a little.

"What's wrong, Paige?" Ezra asked.

"This is delightful," Lucifer said.

"That bitch was eye-fucking you and about to make a grab for your ass. She looks at you like she's had a taste and wants more. No one goddamn touches you."

The room fell silent, except for the rumbling coming from the chest of the man who was holding me. Ezra—I couldn't see him as Azrael since I'd accepted him as being Ezra—turned me in his arms. I tried to keep my gaze on the bitch who looked like she wanted to crawl under the couch, but a hand cupped my cheek, and my head was pried away from her direction to meet with Ezra's warm gaze. Using his free hand, he took mine and brought it up to his chest where I felt the rumbling on his skin. It sounded content.

"She's never had me. She never will because I am yours, if you want me?"

Someone sniffled. However, I couldn't look away from the man in front of me. He was stunning. He was strong. He was a part of Hell, born son of Lucifer. He could be scary and fierce. He was also Ezra, my hellhound who'd I missed with every beat of my heart.

He *was* mine.

I couldn't deny it, and I would never try.

"I will always want you," I told him.

CHAPTER NINETEEN
THORN

Ezra clutched Paige to him and then kissed her like she was his much-needed breath. I couldn't say it hurt seeing it, because it didn't. When Alex and I had been in Hell, we'd spoken of the connection we'd felt with Ezra. The man who refused to go by Azrael because he'd been Paige's Ezra, and that was all he wanted to be. The only ones who refused to call him that were his parents.

Paige jumped, and Ezra caught her with his hands on her sweet ass, holding her tightly to him as they still kissed.

I quickly addressed the room while holding an agitated Nate back. "I think it is time to rest in our rooms."

A beaming Virginia bounced up and clapped her hands, so much like Alma would have done. "Yes, I agree. Let the kids have privacy, Luca."

Lucifer nodded, and, in a blink, he stood by his woman with an arm around her waist. We hadn't seen much of them in Hell, which I was grateful for. I wasn't sure I liked Lucifer, but he was giving his son what he wanted and loved most in his life—Paige. For that, I was grateful. The times we'd seen Virginia in Hell, she'd never once hinted at being Alma. They liked their secrets, which meant we would have to keep a close eye on them. Even when they were being accommodating in helping us with their advice. I had a feeling that had a lot to do with who their son would be bound to, though.

A moan filled the room from Paige when she ground her

crotch against Ezra. He returned it with his own groan, the content rumble in his chest never stopping.

"Out," Lucifer commanded.

I made sure Paige's men were the last to head to the door. Nate still wasn't too pleased to leave. I had to grab a tighter hold of his fur and tug him with me. He licked my hand, pleased I was home, at least that was what I guessed. Immediately after, he went back to growling and fighting my every step. It seemed Nate had claimed Paige and wasn't happy about leaving her with someone his wolf hadn't claimed.

God, I'd missed this, his antics. Actually, I'd missed them all. Alex and I had spoken about home much and how we couldn't wait to be here.

"Wait," a rough, thick voice called.

We turned back to see Ezra helping Paige stand on her shaky feet.

"What is it?" Asher asked. He stood beside me with his hand clasped around Alex's arm. It had been nice knowing Paige had missed us and how much she had, but she hadn't been the only one it seemed.

We were truly a family.

One that had extended to contain Ezra.

Alex and I both knew as soon as Paige found out the truth, she wouldn't let him go. I had been skeptical about Asher and Nate taking it well, but Alex reassured me—for Paige's sake and to see her happy—they would be fine.

"Stay," Ezra said. "You're all Paige's and she's yours. I won't jeopardize anything you already have."

Paige cupped his cheeks, turning his head back to her. Her smile was soft when she pecked his lips. "You're amazing."

He shrugged. "It helps I already know them all and have

felt the connection you have. Though, I'm not sure Nate is too pleased I'm back."

"Nate, shift back." I grunted when he tried to lunge forward again. The bastard was strong; thankfully I nearly matched it.

My hands fell away when his body started to shake. He grew taller and wider. His tail stayed in place when he stopped the shift in his half form.

"Thorn, Asher, you'll have to hold me back until he's claimed her," he growled between sharp, long teeth.

"I've got him," Asher said. He lifted his chin toward Paige. His voice lowered, "Spend time with her."

I shook my head. "But Ezra needs—"

"She needs all three of you."

"Are you sure you can handle him on your own?" Already I wanted to get over to where Ezra guided Paige over to the couch. Even if I liked the feel of Nate against me, where he had my dick hardening, I still felt the pull to go to Paige.

Asher smiled, full fang. "Yes."

Nodding, I dropped my arms. Nate made for Ezra, but Asher was there, throwing him across the room. Asher followed and ignore Nate's snarling and wrapped his arms around Nate from behind, taking him to the floor.

"Settle, pup, and yield for me," Asher demanded.

"Fuck you, vampire." Though, when Asher's legs knocked Nate's apart, Nate's struggles lessened a little. I grinned, understanding dawning on me. Asher had claimed the wolf. I wished I'd been there to see it.

A moan had me looking toward the couch. Ezra watched Alex's hand up Paige's dress. He'd have his fingers inside her, and I wanted to see. Stalking over to them, I stopped and stood before them, crossing my arms over my chest.

"Alex, our mate is dressed in far too many clothes," I said, and caught Alex's grin against Paige's lips. Ezra looked on with desire burning within his eyes and a small smile on his lips.

Alex clicked his fingers. Suddenly, Paige sat on the couch in nothing. Ezra, Alex, and I had only boxers on, all of them tented with our erections. I glanced over to the corner to see Asher was also only in his underwear while he still rolled around on the floor with half-shifted Nate.

A war started up inside me. I wanted to watch everything that was going on, but I couldn't, and when Paige cried out, I moved my gaze quickly back to see her arching as Alex's finger sank deeply into her while Ezra sucked, bit, and licked at her nipple.

Leaning in, I took hold of Paige's thighs and spread her legs apart, hooking one leg over Alex's and then Ezra's. Standing back, I nodded at my good work because now I could see perfectly between her legs. I could see how drenched she was.

Paige whimpered against Alex's mouth before she drew her lips away, turned her head, and kissed Ezra. Alex slipped his finger free and Paige complained, but then his hand glided up her body, took Ezra's hand and moved it down to between her legs.

On his first touch, Ezra's hips jutted forward into Paige's side. Immediately, Paige dropped her hand and slipped it under his boxers to grip him. He groaned harshly into her mouth.

Alex stood from the couch. He grabbed my wrist and roughly pulled me his way. He shifted quickly and pushed me down onto the couch beside Paige.

"Ezra," she whispered. "Please," she begged.

"What?" he bit out, desire riding his demanding voice.

Reaching around her, I took Ezra's chin in hand and forced his burning red gaze, meaning his hellhound side was close, to mine. "She wants you inside her."

His smile was wicked. He nipped at my hand before moving to his knees on the floor.

I glanced down as something dropped to my lap and found a tube of lube. I ripped my gaze up to a cheekily grinning Alex. He rose a brow. Did he seriously think I would knock this option back? I'd been staring at his ass for the last week, wanting to feel it around my cock.

With jerky motions, I lifted my ass, shoved my boxers down, and lathered the lube over my leaking length. Paige had me looking at her when I heard a giggle.

"Yes, sweetheart?"

"I just love to see you all wanting each other." She lifted her chin toward the other men. I caught Asher pushing himself into Nate, who was grinding his teeth together in pleasure. He was refusing to let Asher know he liked being fucked.

My gaze swept back when Alex climbed onto my lap. With a quick glance to Ezra, I was pleased to see he wasn't repulsed by our actions. In fact, he got distracted by Asher fucking Nate. I had a feeling he wanted to take on the wolf as well.

Only, as soon as Paige touched him, Ezra's attention was right back on her. He took her hand, and she gently tugged him closer, between her legs.

"You're mine?" she asked.

"Always."

"It means a connection with all of us," she told him.

He nodded. "Gladly."

"Then you'll accept being my bonded male."

His eyes heated even more. "With pleasure."

"Remove your boxers, mate, and be one with me."

His body shuddered at her words. He pushed down his boxers as Alex cupped the side of my neck, and I lifted my gaze to his. I slid my hands to his waist and then glided them up over his skin to his shoulders, where I could force him down to finish the kiss we'd started in Hell.

He lifted enough to grind his ass down on my cock.

Christ, yes.

A grunted groan had us breaking the kiss, but it didn't stop Alex from rocking over me or me pulling him free from his boxers and jerking him up and down. Before I glanced at Ezra and Paige, I caught Alex biting down on his bottom lip.

Ezra had his head buried in Paige's shoulder. Her eyes were closed, and she panted through the intensity we'd all experienced when finalizing the bond. It also meant Ezra had his cock inside Paige, something I wish I'd seen, but I had my hands full, which I didn't mind at all. They needed their first time private… well, somewhat private.

Alex shifted up, reached through his legs, and gripped my dick. Slowly, he sat with the tip of my cock slipping inside him for the first time.

"Fuck," I clipped.

Alex moaned as he surrounded me with himself. His head dropped back. Leisurely, I reached up and ran my hand from his neck and down. I loved his skin, so much smoother than the rest of us.

Ezra breathed deeply. He picked up his head and stared at Paige in awe. She smiled warmly back at him, wrapping her legs around his waist as he slowly pushed in and out of her.

"You're incredible," he told her, leaning in to nip at her lips. "Unbelievable."

"So are you, my mate, my Ezra, my hellhound."

Nate's cry of release was soon joined with Asher's, but I couldn't look that way. Not when I'd moved my gaze back to Alex, and he'd forced the rest of me inside him with a gasp. His heated eyes met my own. He kissed my chest, my neck. It wasn't enough, not when he started to rock up and down on me. I wrapped an arm around him and gripped his hair to drag his mouth up to mine. We drank each other's moans down. His movements switched to a faster pace.

Purring started over in the corner; Asher's vampire was content.

"Quit it," Nate grumbled.

"No," Asher clipped, never stopping the noise. Alex and I chuckled against each other's mouth, only to stop and glance to Ezra and Paige when Paige cried out.

My hand shot out to grip Ezra's as it lay against the top of her breast. Ezra lifted his head from her shoulder he'd been kissing to glare at me.

"Stop, it's okay," Paige called, and when she smiled, I really knew it was okay. Then, when Paige opened her emotions to all of us, pure ecstasy reached me. I grunted and released my hold on Ezra's arm to grab Alex to me. My balls drew up, and Alex started fucking himself hard, up and down, squeezing my cock each time.

Fuck, he was tight.

"Christ, you feel good," I said against his lips.

"Paige," Ezra yelled. Alex and I looked over, still while he moved over me. Ezra bit out another groaned, "Fuck."

"Yes, hell yes, Ezra," she cried, holding him tightly to her. Her eyes slammed closed as her pleasure peaked, and we all made a noise when we felt her ride over into her orgasm. Ezra growled low, pumping faster; then he made a sound deep within his chest, coming inside our mate before he slowed and slid in and out unhurried.

A small hand snaked between Alex and me. Alex pulled back enough where we could both look down and see Paige's hand stroking Alex's hard cock.

"God, yes," Alex murmured.

I lifted my hand to his face, my thumb to his lips. He drew it into his mouth and sucked on it. I turned my head to claim Paige's mouth. Alex whimpered through his release as it squirted out and onto my chest and stomach. His ass tightened even more, drawing out my own cum into him.

Alex slumped against me, breathing hard. Paige and I broke apart, and my eyes landed on a grinning Ezra, where he rested his head against Paige's chest. I moved my gaze to the top of her breast and caught his handprint burned into her skin. He'd marked her as his, and it didn't bother me because I knew, like all of us did, he was a part of our family.

"I could use a shower, food, and sleep," Nate said from across the room. After I helped Alex off my lap, he clicked his fingers and I felt my skin clean. I wasn't the only one he'd cleaned up either.

"I wouldn't mind feeding," Asher stated, his eyes trained on a blushing Alex from where he and Nate sat leaning against the wall. They'd been watching us and were already hard again.

Remembering Nate being inside me, I couldn't help but want it again since it had been so long.

Nate's eyes also shone with lust.

"We'll go to my room," Paige said, and then she cried out when Ezra swept her up into his arms.

He started for the door, but Paige wouldn't like the thought of all of us naked. I called out, "Alex, clothes please." I heard his click and felt silk against my skin. I started laughing when my body, as well as everyone else's, was covered from chest to feet in silk pajamas.

Happiness had my chest swelling. We were all possessive and protective of one another.

We were perfect together.

CHAPTER TWENTY
PAIGE

As soon as we'd entered my room, Alex had replaced the men's pajamas with boxers, and I was in a short purple see-through teddy. I went straight for the bed and sat on the edge of it. I lifted my gaze from the nightie, smiling. It quickly drifted from my lips, and I bit my bottom one to keep my moan contained, already aroused again. And I wasn't the only one. Watching Asher drink from Alex was erotic in itself, but seeing Alex between Asher's spread legs on the couch and with his hand in Alex's boxers amped up my desire to a new height. I didn't know how I could possibly want more after what we'd just done, but I did, and I knew my males wouldn't deny me.

As I watched Asher and Alex, I didn't even need to ask for attention. Ezra, my newly bonded male, dropped to his knees in front of me, and I shifted my gaze down when he pushed my legs apart.

"I've been wanting a taste for a fucking long time," he said huskily.

Smiling, I reached out and ran a hand through his wild hair. "Who am I to deny you then."

He grinned. Thankfully Alex hadn't put anything but the teddy on my body, so when my legs were wide, Ezra could see how ready I was for him. He groaned and ducked in. On the first swipe of his tongue, I planted my hands on the bed and lifted my pussy to him.

When he sucked on my clit, I cried out, slamming my eyes closed, only to quickly open them and look down at his heated gaze. His tongue swirled around, and then he licked down, flicking his tongue over my entrance.

"Ezra," I whimpered.

"You taste better than I imagined, and I did a lot of that." He kissed my thigh and pushed two fingers inside me. I clamped down around them, causing him to hiss out a breath.

A moan sounded over at the couch. I lifted my hooded gaze and saw Asher had pulled down the front of Alex's boxers. His hand ran up and down Alex's length at a fast pace. Their eyes were on me and Ezra between my legs.

A growl to my left had me searching for my other two males. Nate had Thorn on the floor, on all fours with Nate behind Thorn, fucking him slowly. Their eyes were also on Ezra and me.

Nate grabbed Thorn's shoulder. He pulled him back to wrap his arms around Thorn's chest. Nate kissed Thorn's shoulder as he pumped into Thorn harder, drawing out a ragged groan from my ghoul. God, I loved seeing them together.

I glanced back to Asher and Alex. Alex's arms were holding Asher tightly. His hips ground up and down. I knew he was rubbing his ass against Asher, who licked and nibbled at Alex's neck.

Ezra surged up, his fingers still sliding in and out of me, but when he claimed my mouth, his finger disappeared. I heard a rip and pulled back to look around at my exposed front.

"Fucking stunning, isn't she?"

It pleased me our new member of the family didn't mind what was going on around us. How my other men shared their desires with each other. In fact, as Ezra glanced over to Nate and Thorn, I could sense his lust at their show.

"Christ, yes," Nate said roughly.

Alex and Thorn hummed their approval, and Asher called, "She is, and she's all ours."

I felt Ezra's smile against my breast before he latched his lips around my nipple. Yes, he liked being a part of our family, loved our connection. He was just as special as the rest of them. Something I had always known when he'd been only my hellhound, but more so now that he proved he was my mate and within our fold.

Ezra cupped my other breast and massaged it. I felt his hand between us before the tip of his dick pressed against my entrance.

His mouth went away from my nipple with a pop. He blew cool air over it. "You'll have me inside again?"

"I'll always have you inside me."

He surged forward and embedded deep. I cried out and gripped his shoulders. He buried his head into my neck and rocked in and out of me. I savored his touch, his feel, and already I couldn't wait for the next time with Ezra, even with Asher, Thorn, Nate, and Alex.

"Fuck," Nate clipped. "So goddamn tight," he added just as I caught, even without touching himself, Thorn's cum squirt out the tip and onto the floor. Nate's hand snaked down and tugged on Thorn's cock, drawing more out of him as he bit Thorn's shoulder and grunted through his own release into Thorn.

Seeing it had my walls clamping tighter around Ezra. He groaned, his thrusts more urgent, knowing I was close. My lower belly swirled, and I tipped my head to the other side in time to watch Asher's fangs slide into Alex's neck again. His bite harsh, his eyes green, he was lost in his release against Alex's back. Alex then arched, his cum shooting out and coating his lean stomach and Asher's hand.

"Ezra," I yelled as my orgasm crashed into me. I held Ezra tighter against me and heard his sharp intake of breath before he released inside me.

A woman sure could get used to this.

After we all showered in the actual shower that time, to which I thanked God for my large bathroom, I crawled back into bed. The men moved around the room, some drinking, some eating, while Thorn and Alex spoke of their time in Hell. I listened intently and kept pushing the fear down. They were home. They were safe, I reminded myself.

It was strange yet comforting to see Ezra mold into the family as if he'd always been there. Since his presence was the same, I guessed it made it easy to adjust to him, and in a way, he had been always there, only not in his human form. When he spoke, my other men listened. I could already see the respect they held for him.

Eventually, Alex drifted over to the bed. I opened my arms, and he pulled the sheet back enough to climb in. Rather than lying beside me, he hovered over me until I spread my legs; only then did he rest on me gently. I wrapped my arms around him, and then with one hand, I ran my fingers through his hair. He sighed into my chest.

"Am I too heavy?" he asked groggily. He must have been exhausted since they'd refused to sleep much in Hell. It wasn't that they were scared; they just didn't trust the demons, and I couldn't blame them, even when they had Ezra's protection.

"You're perfect where you are," I told him, and then it didn't take him long before he drifted off. My other men then retired with us. Nate and Ezra close to my sides, while Asher lay behind Nate and Thorn behind Ezra. I'd been blessed with such amazing men in my life. I loved them fully, and I was beyond elated they shared love between each other as well.

Nothing was perfect. I wasn't foolish enough to think what we had would always be sunshine and roses, but I'd enjoy each and every day as they came because my men would be by my side.

"We still have so much to deal with," I said softly into the room. My body tensed just thinking about it all.

"I have been thinking on the matter," Asher said.

"And?" Nate clipped.

"I believe the best way to gain people's attention is, as Lucifer said, to have proof. It is time our queen makes herself known. Not with just the council, but with others."

"What will it gain?" Thorn asked.

"Attention," Ezra added. "If people see what kind of queen Paige is, how respected she is, who she has at her side, others may be willing to listen to Paige and her ways. It will be an asset before things go head-to-head with the council."

"Agreed," Asher said. "I think we need to use the month before seeing the council to our advantage."

Nate grunted. "You're talking about traveling to see other communities, aren't you?"

"Yes. The ones we've heard of. The lost alphas, the fae king, the vampire master, all their people?"

"It could be a good idea," Nate said. "We can speak of our thoughts regarding the council's part in their deaths or disappearances and see where it goes."

"Not everyone will trust," I told them, my stomach

swirling with unease. "It wasn't simple here, and it's not like everything here has been smoothed out with our people. I can still see problems popping up. So how will it be for the other kings or queens who know nothing about me, who have thought the ghouls extinct? Can we really ask them to trust us when the community and my people have been hidden for so long?"

"All we can do is try," Asher said softly.

"It won't be easy," I replied. I felt sick to the gut. I hated the idea, but they made good points. We needed more people with us to go against the council. And if we could get their support, we had a better chance at defeating them.

"No, it won't," Thorn said. "But Asher and Ezra are right. To have others at our back, for people to see the poison within the council, it's best we at least try. If the people we go to, see what we have and witness how the missing or dead rulers have been respected, their replacements—and their people— will do anything to have their missing comrades back and seek vengeance of those kings who died."

"What happens if their replacements are in with the council already?" I questioned.

Thorn's lips thinned. "I'm sure between all of us we will be able to detect such things. Three of your bonded worked with the council for many years. Together, we'll work out who is or isn't to be trusted."

I didn't like the thought of traveling and going into unfamiliar communities, but I believed in my men and their abilities. They would know the rules. They would guide me. All I could do was pray it would lead us to success. I forced myself to relax a little, even when fear for them touched my heart. "What will we use the other month for?" I asked, trying to distract myself.

"Training," Ezra said. "We'll need to make sure we're as strong as we can be."

That was a good idea. We all needed to be at our best for this horrid situation.

"Especially since we'll be going into others' territory," Nate grumbled.

Nerves still fluttered in my stomach. "What about here? Who will take care of the kingdom when we're gone?" I wouldn't leave my people unguarded.

"I'll speak with my parents and see if they will come back while we're gone," Ezra said, and the room quieted.

"They'd do that?" Thorn asked, sounding as surprised as I felt. We were talking about the devil. Though, from what he'd already shown, he wasn't anything like I'd expected. Then again, Ezra was their son, and I was sure that had a lot to do with it.

Ezra chuckled. "My mother has managed to mellow my father in the years they've been together. One thing I am certain of, they would do anything for me... within reason."

"If they're not able to, there is always Felnick and the shifters," Thorn said. They were options, and I knew, if asked, they would do everything within their power to safeguard our land. It still scared me, though, even the thought of asking them because they had their own lives, their own families to take care of.

"Again, there's so much to do," I told them, letting unease seep into them.

Ezra's fingers tickled up my arm before resting his hand flat on my shoulder. "There is, but we'll do it all together." Tipping my head back, he leaned in, knowing what I wanted, and pressed his lips against mine. A little of the panic subsided.

"Agreed," Nate grumbled from my other side. I turned my head his way. He lifted his gaze from Alex, whose head still rested on my naked chest as he softly snored. Nate's lips grazed against mine. More of the fear dashed away.

"We'll protect one another," Asher said from behind Nate. His hand slid over Nate's shoulder, reaching out for me. I removed my hand from Alex's hair and took it.

My men were my world. With them, it had me believing I *could* take on anything.

"We will," I told him. Because I would do anything to keep them all alive.

"Family is always first," Thorn muttered lazily. He got up to his elbow behind Ezra and smiled down at me. "For now, though, sweetheart, let's get some rest."

Laughing, I nodded since my worry was under control. "Rest with all my males sounds like heaven."

Thorn pressed a kiss to the tips of his finger and then moved them to my lips, where I kissed.

Yes, whatever was to come, I would do anything, fight anyone, kill everyone I had to, making sure I would come home with the men I loved. With the family I'd claimed.

Read on for a sneak peek into
A Final Paige.

EXCLUSIVE EXCERPT

PAIGE

"Again," Nate bellowed down at me.

I groaned and rolled to my stomach. Slowly, I clambered to my feet and bared my teeth at him. "You yell at me one more time, I'm going to take your balls from your body."

He snorted, but before he could open his mouth, Thorn said, "I rather like his balls. Maybe take some toes instead, sweetheart."

I shot Thorn the finger, and he chuckled. Until Alex used his power and put him in a bubble. When Thorn started floating up to the roof, his eyes widened. He stumbled around like a fish out of water, cursing up a storm. He pounded at the outer layer, but we all knew nothing would penetrate it. We'd all tried.

My anger disappeared, and I started laughing. But then my feet were knocked out from under me, and I landed with a thump on my back on the floor. Asher stood over me with his hands on his hips.

"Being distracted could get you killed."

"I know," I clipped.

"It could also get someone you love killed," Nate called. I twisted my head to see him standing behind Ezra with his hand around his throat. I knew he wouldn't harm Ezra, but seeing it had me screaming at myself under my breath. They'd been teaching me how to protect myself for the last two weeks, and we'd now moved on to trying to show me how to work within a team. To make sure I not only had myself covered but those who would fight alongside me. I thought I'd made progress, but it was obvious I still had a lot of work to do. My body chilled in worry. I fisted my hands and pressed them against my churning stomach. I wouldn't be ready in time.

We were leaving in two weeks.

Two weeks.

It wasn't enough time.

A sense of failure and worry spread through my veins instead of blood. I didn't want to be the weak link. I had to get better.

Slapping the floor, I stood, ignoring Asher's hand he'd held out to help me.

"Love—" he started, but I shook my head.

I ran a hand over my sweaty face. "Don't give me sweet, encouraging words. I don't want them right now."

He nodded. "All right." He dodged left. I slid right and gripped his arm to take him to the ground, but he was too fast. He easily slipped out of my hold and wound his arm around my throat, pressing his front to my back. I grabbed his hand and bent, flipping him over my body. He landed in a crouch, stood, and turned. His movements were a mere blur with every punch and kick as he drove me backward. I deflected each one.

Out of the corner of my eye, I saw Nate approaching Alex, who still held Thorn in a bubble. I ducked under Asher's punch, unsheathed my blade at my ankle, and threw it across the room; it landed just before Nate's toes.

His gaze hit me, but Alex had also noticed Nate now.

Asher tripped me. I fell on my back, rolled, and jumped up.

He stopped and smiled at me. "Better."

It was a good thing I didn't breathe, or I would have been out of breath. Still, my heart was beating so hard in my chest I was surprised it didn't fall out.

It was wonderful to hear his praise, but I didn't feel it was enough yet. Soon we would be walking into the fae territory, and even though we'd asked for permission and it had been given, I didn't like not knowing what would happen. Actually, all of the meetings we'd set up had been agreed upon since they were all willing to meet with the new ghoul queen. Of course they would want to know if I would be a threat to them and theirs. They'd learn I wouldn't be, unless something happened to someone I claimed as mine.

I'd read up on fae between training, yet the information was limited. And those who had been around the fae told me never to trust them. They were conniving, tricky creatures. They could fly, glamour, and talk their way into your home and bed. I'd heard they were the most stunning creatures in existence, and yes, I'd seen pictures in the books I'd studied. Yet, all I could think was that I saw more beauty in my bonded mates.

I wasn't holding out hope in their help. The fae kept to themselves a lot. For all I knew, the new king, who was the son of the former one, wouldn't care what was going on outside of his kingdom. I had asked why we were even going to see them, but Asher assured me they would be an advantage to have on our side. The council were the ones behind the former king's death. Alex was certain the facts my men already had to show the fae, as well as what they could tell us about that night, would be enough for them to not trust the council and hopefully stand with us. Or if not, then to stay out of the fight when it was time for us to go to them.

Only time would tell.

After the fae kingdom, we were moving on to the two missing alphas. The first was from a lion pride consisting of at least five hundred members. The other was a tiger in charge of his streak. Nate had informed me one night studying that tigers usually didn't group together—they tended to be solitary creatures—but the alpha that had gone missing had been looked up to by many of his kind, which was how he became their leader.

Their groups had also given us permission to enter their territory. However, I had a feeling it could have something to do with wanting to take a good look at the ghoul queen they'd never heard of. Even the fae would want the same, to discover my power and determine if I would be a threat or not.

We had to be careful with how we did things, though, or it could bring us more trouble than just the council.

Lastly, and it was thanks to the woman who'd saved my Asher, we were allowed entry into the deceased master's clan lands to visit the vampires since she'd now taken over as their master. I wasn't looking forward to seeing Cynthia. The interaction Asher had with her concerned me as I could likely kill her if she tried anything. However, Asher told me everything would be fine and Cynthia would listen to what we had to say. It was also likely she'd help us—another thing Asher was sure of. His confidence in her had me wanting to punch her in the face in a fit of jealousy, which was something my men found amusing when they felt and saw how pissed I became every time Asher spoke of her.

Still, I pushed all of that down to worry about when the

time came and, instead, got into a fighting stance. I curled my fingers at Asher and said, "Come at me."

He smirked and then disappeared.

Only that time I brought my powers forward. It helped me see his movement better. Just as he stopped behind me, I twisted, grabbed, and dropped him to his back on the floor. Though, I was sure he allowed it because when I straddled his waist, his hands slowly slid up my thighs. The movement paused, and he rolled me to my back, got to his feet, and crouched in front of me. Nate's growl was pointed at the door, so was Ezra's in his shifted form, and as Thorn's feet touched the floor, he withdrew his sword. Alex, with his delicious power, aimed his glowing-white hands at the door.

It was then I heard it—the heavy footfalls of maybe three people. Quickly, I stood just as the doors to the gym burst open and in them stood a puffing Leon and two of his brothers.

"What's wrong?" I demanded, taking a step forward, until Asher's arm swung out to hold me back.

"Yasmin." My sister's name from his lips had my heart taking off in flight and angst twisting my stomach. He went on. "She was outside with Sophie and two of our brothers. They…." He shook his head.

Jake, Leon's younger brother, continued with "We didn't know the real Sophie was actually inside, since the fake scented the same as the real one. We were all fooled."

Fear grabbed at me. "Then who was Yasmin walking with? Is my sister okay? What happened?"

"We don't know who the imposter was, but the fake Sophie attacked them."

"Where's Yasmin?" I yelled.

Leon's frown said enough, even before he admitted, "We don't know. We have every shifter out searching for her."

I shoved Asher's hand from me and raced from the room. My men followed, as did Leon and his brothers. The guards who'd been outside the gym joined us as well.

"Does Eric know?" Thorn asked.

Leon shook his head. "We kept it quiet. Until…."

"Until we knew more," Jake finished.

"We're sorry we failed you, my queen." Leon's lips thinned. He hated himself, but I couldn't allow it when they would have done everything they could have.

"Your brothers who were with Yasmin?" I asked.

Sorrow crossed his features before he steeled his expression into a blank one. "One didn't make it. The other is with a healer."

We made it outside. Jake pointed at the entryway that led out toward the town behind my castle. I kept moving. "Whoever has done this will pay in flesh and blood," I told him, even knowing it wasn't going to be enough.

Yasmin.

She could be next.

She could die.

I shook my head. I couldn't let that thought settle.

"Thank you, my queen," he said softly.

"Asher?" I called.

He veered left. "Blood, off into the woods."

"That's where our kin were found."

"How do you know Yasmin and Sophie were out here with your brothers in the first place?" I asked, pulling to a stop behind Asher. He lifted his nose and sniffed the area.

"We keep each other informed of all movements. Plus, we questioned a shop owner who they passed. She saw Yasmin and who she thought was young Sophie walk from the castle together with our brothers not far behind. She said she over-heard Sophie saying she wanted to show her mom something."

A trick. Yasmin would follow Sophie anywhere, just like most of us. Only we would have sensed the power used to alter the appearance of whoever was behind this. Though perhaps not since two bear shifters, who had good senses, hadn't. I clenched my jaw and glanced around. Two pools of blood marred the leaves, dirt, and grass. Leon's brothers. My heart ached for them.

Nate and Ezra, who had both shifted at some point, took a few bounds forward and growled. They glanced back, then forward, and took off running. We quickly followed. I hadn't even considered how people would react seeing Ezra back as we'd run through the township and even the castle. He hadn't shifted around anyone but us, and in training only. All they knew was that he was a part of Lucifer's entourage. Lucifer had since left with Virginia and their people, but were coming back when we traveled. It was something to worry about later.

My throat closed as we entered a clearing and I saw Yasmin being held with a knife to her neck by a woman I didn't know.

The woman smiled. "Finally, it took them plenty of time to let you know."

"Who are you and what do you want?" Asher asked.

Nate and Ezra pawed at the ground, snarling from where they stood just in front of me.

"If anyone moves, I will slice her open."

"Answer my mate's questions."

"My queen," a guard called. I glanced to the side as he

stepped forward. "Her name is Tenaya. She is Grace's daughter."

Fuck.

Fuckety-fuck.

Yasmin stared at me with tears in her eyes. Her lips trembled as she smiled sadly at me. She knew this could be it for her. I shook my head slightly, telling her there was still hope. I had my men, the guards. We could kill this bitch without harming my sister.

Dread filled me to the brim. Even with the strength, the magic around me, they were still a distance away. If Tenaya saw Alex disappear, she would kill Yasmin with a quick swipe.

Please, please do not take my sister away from me, from her family. Please.

Another guard moved close. "She is also the one in battle who took her own life."

Tenaya laughed. "Yes, it was so easy to fool you all with all the blood around. So easy to cover the beating of my heart with a spell."

"What do you want?" I pressed. There had to be something she wanted or… no, no, no. It couldn't just be for revenge. I hadn't even remembered her besides when she pretended to take her own life. I'd been so far away, I didn't recognize her. Now closer, I saw the resemblance to Grace.

Her smile was pure evil. "I see the panic in your eyes. You know why we're here."

"Please don't kill her."

"Then you shouldn't have killed my mother."

"She murdered people for power, sent my mates to Hell, conspired with demons," Paige called. "Yasmin is an innocent human being."

Her grip tightened on my sister, and Yasmin whimpered. I fisted my hands. I wanted to tear into the woman. Rip, bite, and kill.

Instead, I locked my body down. Tears welled in my eyes. "Please, please don't kill her. She has a husband, children."

Tenaya smile again. "Oh, I know."

"Why?" I asked on a whisper.

"Because you took my mother," she answered simply.

My eyes connected to Yasmin's. She mouthed, "I love you. Take care of them."

My body shuddered in anguish. "I'll do anything."

"I'm not stupid. We make a bargain, and you'll all kill me in the end—do not move," she yelled. The guards stopped. "All I want is to see your pain, and I have." Quickly, she removed the knife from Yasmin's neck. We all rushed forward. A scream tore out of me when she plunged the knife into Yasmin's chest. Into her heart.

I stumbled. Asher grabbed me. Alex appeared out of nowhere and caught Yasmin as her body sagged. Tenaya stepped back, still grinning, only her eyes widened when Ezra leaped. His mouth surrounded her neck and face. I heard a snap just as Nate joined Ezra, and they shredded her to pieces.

Dropping to my knees beside Alex cradling Yasmin, I reached out and gripped her hand in both of mine. Her hand was loose, no strength evident. A sob caught in my throat. Yasmin gazed up at me as her breath stuttered. Blood spurted from her mouth.

"You t-take care of them," she wheezed.

"No, you'll be here to do it." I shook my head again and again.

"I love you so much…. Not your fault."

I dug my top teeth into my bottom lip. "I love you, but this isn't goodbye. It can't be." Her lips pulled up before she went lax against Alex. "Yasmin," I yelled. "Please, please, Yasmin."

Hands dropped to my shoulders. "She's passed out, love. Just passed out."

I lifted my gaze and looked at Alex and Thorn. When Nate pressed himself between them, I met his gaze. Finally, I glanced at Asher. "Get Eric," I ordered.

"Sweetheart, are you sure—"

"Get Eric, now!" I bellowed. Asher disappeared, and the warm breeze blew over us.

I wouldn't—couldn't lose my sister… but if Eric didn't agree, then I would have to say goodbye, and that thought had me trembling in fear.

Ezra, still in his hellhound form, moved to my side. I ignored the blood around his mouth and curled an arm over his neck, pulling him close. Thorn went to his knee on my other side, Nate trotted around to my back and pressed in, while Alex laid his hand over mine still clutching Yasmin's.

I wasn't sure their support and comfort would be enough for what was to come, but I appreciated it all the same. They would be the only reason I got through this.

MORE BOOKS
Titles under L.Rose

Hidden Kingdom Trilogy

A Torn Paige

A Lost Paige

A Final Paige (releasing February 2020)

MORE BOOKS
Titles under Lila Rose

Romance

Hawks MC: Ballarat Charter

Holding Out (FREE)

Climbing Out

Finding Out (novella)

Black Out

No Way Out

Coming Out (m/m novella)

(They're also available in box sets in KU)

Hawks MC: Caroline Springs Charter

The Secret's Out

Hiding Out

Down and Out

Living Without

Walkout (novella)

Hear Me Out (m/m)

Breakout (novella)

Fallout

(They're also available in box sets in KU)

Romantic Comedies

Making Changes

Making Sense

Fumbled Love

Paranormal

In The Dark (standalone)

ABOUT THE AUTHOR

Find L.Rose online
www.lilarosebooks.com/
Facebook:
bit.ly/2du0taO
Instagram:
instagram.com/lilarose78
email: lilarose2678@gmail.com